W9-APN-838

THE
PALACE
GUARD

Interboro Public Library
802 Main St.
Peckville, PA 18452

860262

THE PALACE GUARD

Charlotte MacLeod

Thorndike Press • Thorndike, Maine

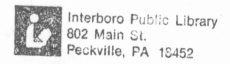

Interboro Public Library
802 Main St.
Peckville, PA 18452

Library of Congress Cataloging in Publication Data:

MacLeod, Charlotte.
    The palace guard.

    1. Large type books.   I. Title.
[PS3563.A31865P34   1981b]   813'.54   81-23218
ISBN 0-89621-345-5   AACR2

For Charlotte Hunnewell Lamson

At the time of writing, the Fenway Studios still exists in its originally intended form, as an ideal place for artists to work.

For the sake not only of those dedicated people who are trying to preserve the building as it should be, but for all the artists who have toiled there over the years to enrich Boston's cultural heritage, this writer fervently hopes the Fenway Studios' unique aesthetic and architectural value will be recognized and cherished.

The two tenants described in this story are, of course, imaginary. So is the Madam's palazzo, as nobody in real life was ever foolhardy enough to try to outshine the incomparable Mrs. Jack. There isn't even a Tulip Street on the Hill. Sarah Kelling, her boarders, her friends, and her foes have nowhere to exist except in the author's imagination. No resemblance to any actual person or event is intended, and any coincidence would be inadvertent.

CHAPTER 1

The burst of well-bred applause dwindled to a spattering of claps from the young cellist's more dedicated relatives, then was drowned altogether in the scraping of chairs. The tourists moved toward the exit at the rear of the concert hall. The cognoscenti pressed forward into the Tintoretto Room, to partake of white wine and cheese, say nice things to the musicians, and dodge candle drippings from Madam Eugenia Wilkins's famous cinquecento chandeliers.

Mr. Max Bittersohn, distinguished young art expert, seized the elbow of his remarkably attractive young landlady, Mrs. Sarah Kelling of the Beacon Hill Kellings. "Let's get the hell out of this," he hissed. "That kid who's been slaughtering Boccherini has more sisters and cousins and aunts than a chorus line from *Pinafore.*"

Sarah, who had been brought up in a sterner school, demurred. "We mustn't leave without at least speaking to your friend Mr. Fieringer. You know he's always heartbroken if you don't say something about his latest genius."

"What's to say? Okay, then, come out on the balcony till the crowd thins a little."

"I did think the pianist managed beautifully, all things considered."

"Yes, old Bernie's a damn fine musician still, on the rare occasions when he can find his way to the piano. I wonder how Nick managed to keep him sober for the occasion."

"Heavens, what an impresario must go through." Sarah rested her dainty forearms on the carved marble balustrade and looked down at the enclosed courtyard, now massed with spring flowers for Eastertide, or, as in Mr. Bittersohn's case, Passover. "Look, isn't this fantastic?"

On January 1, 1903, Eugenia Callista Wilkins, widow of a railroad baron, had attended the opening of Fenway Court, better known to Boston as Mrs. Jack Gardner's Palace. Seething with what she told herself was scorn, she vowed to show Mrs. Jack how it should have been done. She had then followed the other woman's example by sailing for Europe with her own tame art expert in tow, loaded a Cunarder's hold with an even bigger and more ill-assorted collection of art treasures true and false, come home and built an even more pretentious palazzo on the picturesque banks of the romantic Muddy River, and there arranged her purchases in even wilder confusion.

Mrs. Wilkins had explained to the dumbfounded architect that her indoor garden must have a waterfall full three stories high to plash down over a series of marble basins into a lily pool stocked with exotic fishes. She would have even more flower beds than Mrs. Jack, to be kept ever blooming with stock from even more greenhouses. She would have mosaic walks alleged to have been spirited away during the restoration of Herculaneum and she would have real, live white peacocks fanning their spectacular tails hither and yon as the spirit moved them.

In practice, the peacocks were more apt to be molting, committing nuisances on the mosaics, pecking fretfully at the ankles of visitors, or coming down with various avian ailments and having to be rushed to the Angell Memorial Hospital for treatment. Despite their perverse behavior, though, Mrs. Wilkins' palazzo was generally conceded to be quite a place, even for Boston.

The Kellings, being among Old Boston's

richest, most prolific, and sometimes most respected families, had attended the 1911 opening in droves. It was upon that historic occasion a then Mrs. Alexander Kelling had observed with that tact and courtesy for which the Kellings were noted that the place looked less like an Italian palazzo than a Babylonian bordello. Some other wit had immediately started calling Mrs. Wilkins the Madam, and the name stuck. Making the best of a bad business, Eugenia Callista had thenceforth ordered her visiting cards engraved "Madam Wilkins" but she had never left one on a Kelling.

Even after she died and bequeathed her estate to the city as a museum, therefore, the Kellings had stayed away from the Madam's. It was with an agreeable feeling of tasting forbidden fruit that Sarah gazed down at a molting peacock. For some reason the courtyard was quite empty at the moment except for the birds, the fish in the lily pond, and a bored-looking guard leaning against a pillar. The babble from the Tintoretto Room sounded pleasantly far away. The early April sun slanted down through the vast skylights. Sarah blinked and yawned.

Bittersohn smiled down at her. "Sleepy, Mrs. Kelling?"

They were still on last-name terms as befitted a lady five months widowed and a gentleman who had been lodging with her only since January, but somehow Mr. Bittersohn had developed a way of saying "Mrs. Kelling" that made Sarah feel her unmarried status. And he did seem to get a great many free passes to concerts and plays that he thought perhaps she'd like to attend with him if she had nothing better to do and somehow she never did have. It was rather fun to go places after the austere life she'd lived with a husband more than twice her age, and Alexander himself would have been the last person in the world to think she should let a free pass go to waste. So even though this hadn't been a good concert, she smiled back.

"It's that warm sun, and the smell of the flowers. This really is a delightful place. I do wonder, though, why the Madam thought it would be more cultured to put such hard chairs in the music — look!"

Something large and dark hurtled past them, to crash among the pink and purple hyacinths two stories below. A peacock and a guard screamed together. Bittersohn was down the marble staircase before the echoes died.

Sarah rushed after him as fast as her high heels and clinging skirt would let her. She could see the crumpled thing in the garden now. It was one of the palazzo's guards, his green uniform looking strangely harmonious with the green foliage. The courtyard guard was sweating, frantic, putting up a valiant single-handed battle to keep back the crowd that had appeared where nobody had been a moment before.

"Stand back, please," he was shouting. "Sir, you can't — "

"I'm a doctor," said Bittersohn. Actually his doctorate was in fine arts, but it did the trick. Spectators fell back. The guard breathed a sigh of relief. Bittersohn bent over the body.

"Fractured skull and a broken neck," he pronounced. "Who is he, do you know?"

"Sure." The live guard wet his lips. "I'd know him just from the shabby uniform. That's Joe Witherspoon, oldest guy in the place. Been here since Curley was mayor."

"Then how come he didn't know enough to stay away from the railings?" cracked some bright soul in the crowd.

The guard shook his head. "Beats me. Joe shouldn't have been out on the balcony at all. His station's in the Titian Room, on the third floor. Long way for an old man to climb, but Joe wouldn't change. I'm surprised he'd leave his girl friend alone for a minute with so many visitors around today."

"What do you mean, leave his girl friend?" asked Bittersohn.

The guard emitted a snort of embarrassed laughter. "That's what we call the big Titian, the 'Rape of Lucrece.' We always kid Joe about being soft on Lucrece, see? Used to, I mean."

By now several other guards had arrived and the first one eased himself away from the body. "Between you and me, Doctor, I think Joe was kind of soft in more ways than one. Ask the guys here."

The guys didn't seem inclined to answer, so the spokesman went on. "See, we've got this locker room down in the basement, where we keep our stuff and maybe grab a smoke during our coffee breaks. So I go down yesterday afternoon and I see Joe sitting there with his head in his hands, not saying anything. I think maybe he's taking a little nap sitting up like some people do, so I have my coffee and rest my feet awhile. Then my time's up, so I go to leave, but Joe's still sitting. So I say, 'What's the matter, Joe? How come you're not in a rush to get back to your girl friend?' So he says,

'That's not her any more. She ain't the same. She's gone.' Now, does that make any sense to you?"

To an art expert whose specialty was thefts and forgeries it made all the sense in the world. "Is the picture different in any way?" Bittersohn inquired mildly.

"Of course it isn't. I went up and took a look for myself."

"You feel you know the Titian well enough to spot any alteration?"

"Well, sure, I've covered for Joe enough times. Besides, it's the kind of picture a guy really looks at, if you get me."

"I get you. Why don't you go and find out whether the police have been called? Tell the guard at the door not to let anybody in or out till they get here. The police will want to ask a few questions, no doubt." Bittersohn surveyed the crowd, now really swelled by the influx from the Tintoretto Room. "Good luck to them."

He stood up and looked around for Sarah, who managed to wriggle her way to his side. "Do you think there's something fishy about this?" she murmured.

"I don't know. It seems an odd sort of accident for a guard to have, unless he leaned over to get a look at something down here and lost his balance. He was old, he might have had dizzy spells."

"But there was nothing to see, particularly. Don't you recall how empty the garden was just then? He fell from right over our heads, so he wouldn't have seen anything we didn't."

"That's true. But he screamed or something, didn't he?"

"No, I think that was the peacock. And this other guard yelled at the same time. I don't believe Witherspoon made any sound at all."

The courtyard guard corroborated Sarah's observation. He hadn't actually seen Joe come over the balustrade, but he'd looked up when the peacock screamed and seen the body hit the ground. He probably had yelled something or other. He didn't remember hearing Joe make any sound. That didn't surprise him. Joe had never been much of a talker.

"Come on, Mrs. Kelling." Bittersohn appeared by now to have acquired quasi-official status. At any rate, while the guards were blocking anybody else from going upstairs, they didn't try to stop him and Sarah. There were still a few people straggling down from the Tintoretto Room, but by the time the two approached the third floor, they had the broad marble staircase to themselves. Even the second-floor guards had left their stations to help control the melee in the courtyard.

"What a time to pull a snatch," Bittersohn remarked. "Not one damn thing being watched. No, by George, I'm wrong. The boy's still on the burning deck."

"Who?" Glad of a chance to pause and catch her breath, Sarah looked around. "Oh, you mean that cute little guard over there under the fake Romney. Why, it's Cousin Brooks!"

She darted across the vast foyer that Madam Wilkins had dubbed the Grand Salon and filled with sedan chairs and suits of armor that couldn't possibly have ever fit anyone. "Cousin Brooks, whatever are you doing here?"

"Good afternoon, Sarah." The elderly man greeted her warmly without relaxing his vigil a jot. "How nice you look in that blue outfit. I always liked it on your mother. You're growing into a very pretty young lady."

"About time, don't you think? I'll be twenty-seven next month."

"Good heavens. And Jem tells me you've turned your place into a boardinghouse. I was sorry about poor Alex. Can't remember if I ever got around to telling you so."

"Yes, you wrote a lovely letter. From South Dakota, I believe it was. You were lecturing on your Indian relics."

"So I was. Now I'm doing programs of bird calls at children's parties. In case — er — " He looked questioningly at Bittersohn.

Sarah blushed. "Oh, I beg your pardon. This is one of my boarders, Mr. Max Bittersohn. Brooks is another Kelling, needless to say, and I can't remember how we're related and I haven't the faintest idea what he's doing here."

"We're fourth cousins twice removed and I'm obliging a lady friend. Did you say Bittersohn, sir?"

"I didn't but she did, and I am."

"Not the Max Bittersohn who tracked down old Thaddeus's Corots for him? I knew I'd met you somewhere. I was your prime suspect for a while, wasn't I? Delighted to see you again, sir." Brooks pumped Bittersohn's hand as enthusiastically as if they'd been old lodge buddies. "Dash it, sir, this is the pleasantest surprise I've had since I spotted a Hudsonian godwit flying over the Hatch Memorial Shell just two degrees northeast of Harry Ellis

Dickson. May I make so bold as to ask whether you're on my trail again? Has there been hugger-mugger among the Murillos?"

"Damned if I know." Bittersohn was enjoying the reunion, too. "All I can tell you is that a guard named Joe Witherspoon took a header off the balcony about three minutes ago and landed in the hyacinths. Know anything about it?"

"So that's what all that commotion in the courtyard is about. I've been wondering."

"Haven't you gone to look?"

"Certainly not. How would I know the diversion was not deliberately staged to lure me from my appointed post? I knew Witherspoon, of course. He ought to have been in the Titian Room, over there." Kelling pointed across the Grand Salon. "What was he doing on the balcony?"

"I was hoping you could tell me."

"Believe me, sir, I should be proud and happy to assist you were it in my power. I last saw Joe when I came on duty just before the museum opened, which is at one o'clock on Sundays as you perhaps know. I stuck my head in to explain that I was taking the place of Jimmy Agnew, who would normally be here today. Joe seemed his usual self then."

20

"You didn't see him come out of the Titian Room?"

"I did not. My view, as you can see for yourself, is obscured by the presence of all those ratty old broken-down sedan chairs Mrs. Wilkins saw fit to clutter the place up with."

"Did he look depressed when you spoke with him?"

"Joe always looked depressed."

"Did he happen to mention the big Titian? Did he tell you there was something wrong with it?"

"Sir," said Brooks Kelling warmly, "there's nothing wrong with 'Lucrece.' My one poignant and burning regret is that I've never met one built like her, else I should not be a lonely bachelor today. Had Joe made any such remark I should have refuted it with some heat, but he didn't. He didn't say much of anything to me. If he talked to anyone, it would have been more apt to be Brown, who's supposed to prowl about the corridors looking magisterial. Brown should have seen Joe fall if any of us did." He raised his voice. "Brown? Brown?"

Nobody answered.

"Perhaps he's gone downstairs," Sarah suggested. "Or, wait, someone's coming now."

"That's not Brown," said her cousin fretfully as another guard threaded his way among the sedan chairs. "That's Vieuxchamp and he ought to back with the Uccellos. What are you doing away from your station, Vieuxchamp?"

"Relax, Kelling. Nobody's left on this floor and the police aren't letting anybody up. Who's this, and why are you yelling for Brownie?"

"This is Mr. Bittersohn and he wants to ask Brown who shoved Joe Witherspoon over the balustrade."

"Shoved? Christ, I never thought of that." Vieuxchamp wheeled and headed for one of the archways. "I'll search the corridors. You look in the chapel. Brownie? Hey, Brownie!"

CHAPTER 2

It was Sarah who found the missing guard.
He was flat out under a twelfth-century choir
stall with his eyes closed, moaning softly.
Cousin Brooks whipped out an ammonia am-
pul and crushed it under the man's nose.
Brown choked, spluttered, and tried to sit up,
but he was a fat man and too tightly wedged
in. Brooks and Max Bittersohn had to move
the massive carved oaken bench to get him
out. Vieuxchamp, who claimed to have a
double hernia, contributed to the effort only
insofar as to demand, "How the hell did you
manage to get stuck under there?"

"I don't know," Brown replied woozily. "I
was making my rounds like always and
somebody jumped me. Is anything missing?"

"Yeah, Joe Witherspoon. He went over the
balcony and busted his skull open. Brains all
over the courtyard," Vieuxchamp added with
what Sarah thought was decidedly misplaced
enthusiasm.

"You don't say! What'd Joe do, take a dizzy spell or – oh." Brown clambered to his feet. "I get it."

The chapel was lighted only by a rack of votive candles. It took the others a moment to spot the jumble of church silver lying beside the altar.

"Look at that, will you? They were trying to steal the silver. I came along and they slugged me and shoved me under the pew. Joe heard the noise and came to see what was happening, so they pitched him over the balustrade to shut him up. Then they realized what they'd done and decided they'd better scram without the loot."

"That doesn't sound awfully reasonable to me," Sarah said. "Why would anybody take all those bulky chalices and whatnot in broad daylight with the place full of visitors? They might have known they'd never get away with it."

"They melt it down."

"Where? Over those little votive candles?"

"Lady, how do I know? I'm only telling you what must have happened."

"Good of you," grunted Bittersohn. "Vieuxchamp, would you mind going down to the courtyard and asking somebody from the police to come up here? Brown, what makes you so sure Witherspoon would have heard a disturbance in the chapel? The Titian Room's all the way over on the opposite side of the Grand Salon, isn't it?"

"Yeah, but — "

"You didn't see him away from his post?"

"Not that I recall."

"Was he in the habit of wandering around?"

"Joe? Not usually, but there's always the off chance, isn't there? Or maybe the crooks ran in there after they slugged me, and Joe saw their faces and they panicked and killed him. How do I know? I was out like a light."

"You keep saying they, Brown. How many of these silver thieves were there?"

"Jeez, I don't know. Two or three maybe."

"What makes you so sure there was more than one if you never saw them?"

"I must have heard their footsteps behind me."

"Then why didn't you turn around?"

"Look, who the hell are you, anyway? Get off my back. I got a headache. I'm not saying another word till the cops get here."

The injured guard planted himself on the wormholed bench, set both large feet firmly on the tessellated floor, and buttoned his flabby lips into a surprisingly thin line. The others stood around watching him sit until a harassed-looking man in a wrinkled raincoat toiled up the three long flights of the Grand Staircase.

"Oh, Christ, Bittersohn, you here?" was his amiable greeting. "I knew I should never have got up this morning. Hanging around the nudes again, eh?"

"May I call your attention to the fact that there's a lady present?" said Bittersohn with great dignity. "Mrs. Kelling, may I present Lieutenant Davies."

"How do you do?" Sarah held out her hand. "It seems odd we haven't met. I thought I knew everyone on the force by now."

"Oh, you're that Mrs. Kelling?" Lieutenant Davies shook the small hand carefully, as if he were afraid it might come off. The way things had been happening among the Kellings lately, one never knew. "I've been wondering why the guys are all in love with you."

"Are they? How charming of them. I must explain that I'm merely an innocent by-stander this time. Mr. Bittersohn had passes to the concert and he offered me one."

"Not bad, Bittersohn, considering the concerts are free and therefore no passes are issued."

"Thanks, Davies. Remind me to do you a favor sometime. Speaking of concerts, this gentleman on the bench has a song on his lips. He wants to sing it to you. He doesn't like me."

"Who does? Stick around, will you?"

"Sure. Mind if I get Mrs. Kelling's cousin here to show us some of the priceless art treasures? I'd like to get a look at the big Titian."

"Naturally you would," said Brooks. He led the way with alacrity. Perhaps it had been Titian who painted this particular version of a popular subject, perhaps it hadn't. In any event, Lucrece appeared to be taking her ravishment like a trouper. Even through half an inch of dust and old varnish, the lady was quite an eyeful.

"I suppose she's all right if you like fat women," Sarah sniffed. "Mr. Bittersohn, would it be in order to ask why you were so hard on that guard Brown?"

"Because Brown is a liar, and a damned poor one. He claims he was struck from behind, but we found him lying on his back. He was wedged under that bench so tight that we had to lift it to get him out. So the alleged burglars who were in such a hurry to get away that they dumped their loot took the time to turn him over, lift that heavy choir stall, and plunk it down on top of him. Or else he sucked in his fat gut and used his hands to shove himself in under the bench without help."

"But why would he do that?"

"Maybe he saw Witherspoon thrown over the railing, got scared, and hid. Maybe he did the throwing himself and is trying to fake an alibi. Maybe the killer happened to be a pal of his and told him to make himself scarce so he wouldn't get involved."

Brooks Kelling nodded his neat gray head. "Exactly the sort of perspicacious observation I expected from you, Bittersohn. Of course Brown's telling fairytales. Even Sarah pointed out the absurdity of anyone's trying to steal church silver on a busy Sunday afternoon. Brown undoubtedly piled the stuff there himself. No doubt he left fingerprints, but they won't count, because he can always say he handled the silver in the line of duty."

"How would you describe Brown, Kelling?"

"Fat. Fat in the body and fatter in the head. Stupid enough to let somebody use him. Too stupid to make an effective accomplice. I would guess that somebody instructed him to fake a robbery and pretend to have been attacked, but forgot to remind him that people who get hit on the backs of their heads are more apt than not to fall on their faces."

"Does anyone around here have brains?"

"Mr. Fitzroy, the superintendent, is a man of considerable acumen. He happens to have been on a short holiday this week, a circumstance that may not be without significance. Vieuxchamp shows occasional glimmerings of intelligence. Jimmy Agnew, the man whose place I'm taking, does not. Melanson wouldn't dare think without permission."

"Who's Melanson?"

"The spiritual heir of Caspar Milquetoast. He's stationed among the Italian pottery at the rear on this floor. Nobody in his or her right mind would ever steal those atrocities, but Melanson lives in constant dread lest some militant aesthete rush in with a club and smash the collection in the interest of a more beautiful Boston. I'm sure he's still at his post. He won't leave until somebody tells him he may."

"Then let's go see him. What's wrong with Agnew?"

"Allegedly he has a bug. In fact he's no doubt suffering from an overdose of Schenley's."

"How did you get elected to fill in?"

29

"Jimmy's sister Dolores volunteered me. Dolores and I are old friends."

"What does Dolores Agnew have to do with appointing the guards?"

"She's Dolores Agnew Tawne, widowed since God knows when. Dolores is the oil on the squeaking hinge around here, as one might say. She cleans the paintings, dusts the statues, polishes the silver, doctors the peacocks, hectors the gardeners, arranges the flowers, lights the candles in the chapel, and whatnot. I expect her influence is all that keeps Jimmy on the job. He's an agreeable enough chap but not what one would describe as a zealous worker. Dolores is the salt of the earth."

Sarah knew what that meant: a loud voice and plenty of beef to the heel. Brooks had always been the natural prey of bullying women.

They stopped to tell Davies where they were going, and he elected to come, too. The wretched Melanson was found cowering among his preposterous bibelots. When he saw them he jumped about a foot.

"Oh! Oh, thank goodness it's you, Mr. Kelling. Isn't this dreadful? Vieuxchamp was just telling me — " He stammered "dreadful" another time or two, then petered out.

"Can you tell us anything, Mr. Melanson?" Davies asked him.

"Heavens to goodness, no. Nothing at all. I didn't know a thing until Vieuxchamp told me."

"Haven't you heard all the noise from the courtyard?"

"I couldn't very well help that, could I? I knew something dreadful must have happened."

"But you didn't go to look?"

"How could I? We're not allowed to leave our stations. Mr. Fitzroy is very strict on that point. Vieuxchamp shouldn't have come here. I hope you don't think I lured him in?"

"That's all right, Mr. Melanson. The police have the floor sealed off. Have you any idea why anybody might want to murder Joe Witherspoon?"

Davies' question threw the timid soul into an utter tizzy. "B-burglars," he stammered. "Vieuxchamp said it was burglars. It must have been burglars. Mustn't it?"

"Why? I don't recall any robberies being reported from here."

"Oh no, we've never had a robbery before. Not," Melanson amended hastily, "that I know of."

"Do you suspect there may have been a theft that was never exposed?"

"Gracious, no, I wouldn't dream of suspecting any such thing. But if it should ever turn out there had been and I'd said there wasn't, somebody might think – "

"Mr. Melanson," Bittersohn interrupted, "do you recall ever having heard Witherspoon complain that something had been changed?"

"About the two Uccellos, you mean? No, I believe that was Mr. Fitzroy. I may be wrong, of course, but I'm quite sure it was Mr. Fitzroy who spoke to Mrs. Tawne. Almost sure, that is. Well, fairly sure."

"And what did Mr. Fitzroy say to Mrs. Tawne?"

"Please don't think I deliberately listened. But Mr. Fitzroy wasn't mincing his words, I can tell you that. I suppose it's all right for me to tell you. I mean, it's not as if he – that is, it was Mrs. Tawne who – "

"Who what?"

"Who hung them the other way around because she thought they'd look better that way. After Madam Wilkins left explicit instructions, too! It was – was – " Words failed him.

"As you must know, Bittersohn, the

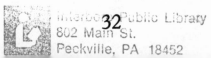
Interboro Public Library
802 Main St.
Peckville, PA 18452

Madam's will stipulated that everything must be left exactly as she placed it," Brooks Kelling took it upon himself to explain. "Madam Wilkins had phenomenally atrocious taste."

"That's right," Melanson was happy to agree. "And there they were, if you please, hanging face to face when they'd always hung back to back. I saw them myself."

"When was this?"

"About — let me see — it was when I had the carbuncle, I do know that. Perhaps three, no four — oh, dear, it's so difficult. I'd say it must have been roughly four years ago last October but I couldn't tell you for sure."

Bittersohn sighed. "You don't recall a more recent incident?"

"I should hope that sort of thing wouldn't happen often!"

Vieuxchamp's reappearance kept Sarah from disgracing herself by a fit of the giggles. "I've been checking around," he explained. "As far as I can tell offhand, nothing's been taken. We'd have to do it with the inventory list to be sure."

"Who keeps the list?" asked Lieutenant Davies.

"Mr. Fitzroy. He'll be here tomorrow morning."

"Who's in charge when he's not around?"

"I guess you might say we all are. Each guard is responsible for his own station."

"Mr. Fitzroy is an unusual man," Brooks interjected. "He believes in the dignity of the individual."

"Besides," said Vieuxchamp, "we're all too scared of him to foul up. Aren't we, Milky?"

"We all have the greatest respect for Mr. Fitzroy," said Melanson primly.

"God help Brown when Fitzy finds out he almost let somebody get away with the communion plate," Vieuxchamp went on. "Brownie's lucky he got that crack on the head. It just might be considered an extenuating circumstance, that and poor old Joe's getting killed."

"Then you go along with Brown's theory that Witherspoon was murdered to keep him from being able to identify the alleged thieves?" said Bittersohn.

"Well, yeah, I guess so. It makes sense, doesn't it?"

Bittersohn didn't point out that it made sense only if one accepted Brown's clumsy pretense of robbery. If, as Brooks Kelling claimed, Vieuxchamp had occasional glimmerings of intelligence, why was he so willing to swallow the story?

CHAPTER 3

"Then you don't believe Witherspoon could have either jumped or fallen?"

Bittersohn's question appeared to give Vieuxchamp some trouble. "Why would he jump?"

"The guard down in the courtyard maintains Witherspoon was upset over some change he either saw or fancied in the big Titian he was so fond of."

"Oh, that? Hell, a man wouldn't kill himself over a painting. I suppose he could have fallen, now that you mention it. See, there's that big clock over the main exit. You can't see it from the third floor unless you lean over the balustrade. Sometimes we do, to see if it's time for our coffee break or something. Joe might have been doing that and taken a dizzy spell and lost his balance."

"I didn't know Witherspoon had dizzy spells," Melanson said interestedly.

"Oh, sure, had 'em all the time. Harden-

35

ing of the arteries, I suppose. Joe was no kid, you know."

"Speaking of getting along in years, Mrs. Kelling, we'd better go see if we can find Nick Fieringer. He'll be wondering why we never showed up in the Tintoretto Room after the concert." Bittersohn got behind Brooks Kelling and went through a pantomime that Sarah at last managed to interpret as "Ask him to supper."

She couldn't imagine why, but she obeyed. "Cousin Brooks, it's been such ages since we've seen each other that I hate to say good-bye. Can't you drop over to the house after you go off duty? It's always an informal buffet on Sunday nights because I never know who's going to be around."

"Why, that's kind of you, Sarah, and I'd like to come. As it happens, however, I'm bespoken. I've already invited Dolores Tawne to eat with me. At that little café over on Huntington Avenue near the Art Museum," he added thriftily.

"Then why don't you bring her along? I'm sure we'd enjoy meeting her."

Sarah wasn't at all sure but she thought she must have said the right thing, because Mr. Bittersohn was looking pleased. Cousin Brooks, on the other hand, demurred. He was afraid Dolores might interpret an invitation to meet the family as a sign of serious intent. Sarah argued that one fourth cousin twice removed and an assortment of paying guests could hardly be interpreted as serious intent. Brooks, seeing both the force of her argument and a chance to save a few dollars, for he was, after all, a Kelling, finally agreed.

"I hope I did what you wanted," Sarah remarked to Bittersohn as they left the group and started downstairs to the second floor, where it was possible Nick Fieringer might still be waiting.

"You did fine," he said somewhat abstractedly, staring at the head of a petulant-looking Heracles.

"What are you thinking?" she prodded.

"I'm thinking that, as Diamond Jim Brady said to the Floradora Girl, there's deception behind that bust. How did you know the Romney's a fake?"

"Because my Aunt Emma out in Longmeadow owns the original. She's an ancestress of ours and I'm supposed to resemble her, though I can't see it myself."

"Did Madam Wilkins know your family owned the original?"

"I doubt it. They were never on visiting

terms, especially after the debacle at the opening. If anything was said then, I'm sure she insisted hers was the original and ours the copy, but it can't be unless Romney painted two identical pictures of the same subject. I'm quite sure he didn't. That's the sort of thing Aunt Emma would know about. I could take you out to see Aunt Emma's by way of comparison if you like."

Bittersohn's lips twitched, and Sarah knew why. If Cousin Brooks was nervous about finding himself romantically compromised on the strength of a short subway ride and a supper of cold roast beef and tapioca pudding in well-assorted company, what would Aunt Emma think of Sarah's driving all the way to Longmeadow à deux with a remarkably attractive man of suitable years and substantial income?

"I'd like very much to see the original sometime," he replied, "but I don't need that to convince me. So far just about everything I've seen in this place is a fake. Either Madam Wilkins was the prize patsy of all time or there's a large rat i' the arras."

"The arras being bogus also, I presume? Is that why you asked me to invite Cousin Brooks? Surely you don't think he's involved in some art forgery racket? Did you really suspect him that time about Uncle Thaddeus' Corots?"

"The answers are no, no, and no, in that order. Your cousin's a bit of a screwball in some ways if you don't mind my saying so —"

"Why should I? Show me a Kelling who isn't."

"But, as I was about to remark, he's nobody's fool, he's fun to be with, and as far as I know he's so honest it's ridiculous. I simply want to talk to him. I'll owe you a meal to make up for him and his lady friend."

"You will not. Owe it, I mean. Of course if somebody happens to give you a free pass to the Ritz." Sarah showed a dimple that was an agreeable surprise in her squarish, clear-skinned but pale face, and Bittersohn laughed.

"So!" a bass voice unctuous as beef drippings exploded. "This is where I find you, Bittersohn. Canoodling among the cupids with a beautiful lady instead of in the Tintoretto Room telling my talented young protégée she should maybe learn her scales before she thinks Carnegie Hall."

"Hi, Nick. Mrs. Kelling and I were on our way to find you."

"I believe you," said the fat impresario archly. "Maybe you can tell me how come the cops in the courtyard? So my young genius takes her cadenzas like a case of whooping cough, is she under arrest for disturbing the peace?"

"Nick, the kid was fine. She needs a little more practice. Tell me, how well do you know the guards in this place?"

"I know everybody." That was a simple statement of fact. Nicholas Fieringer did, almost.

"What sort of man was Joe Witherspoon?"

"Was? Why was? Has something happened to Joe?"

"He landed on his head in the courtyard just about the time your young genius must have been making her curtsey to Mrs. Forbot."

"Old Joe?"

The impresario was one of those large, squashy, bald men whose emotions are close to the surface. His mouth puckered like a baby's. Sarah would not have been surprised if he'd burst into loud wails. After a moment, though, he went on calmly enough. "I can think of nothing more unlikely. How could this happen?"

"The corridor guard on the third floor

claims somebody tried to rob the chapel. Brown, his name is. You know him, too, I expect. Anyway, Mrs. Kelling here found him stuffed under a choir stall with a bunch of silver cups and stuff in a heap by the altar. His story is that two or three guys slugged him during an attempted robbery and pitched Witherspoon over the balustrade to protect their identities."

"Brown is a fraud and a fake! In the concert hall we had eighty-seven people. Always I count first thing before they start tiptoeing out. In other rooms must have been maybe a hundred more. The chapel is on the third floor. The Grand Staircase is the only way to go up and down unless you lower a rope in broad daylight from a window in front of everybody walking dogs and using pooper-scoopers on the sidewalk, *quod erat absurdem*. Down the Grand Staircase to lug a sackful of silver in front of so many people who could believe? Who could believe a liar like Brown if he swore on a genuine Gutenberg Bible which, *entre nous,* you will not find here. Brown sneaks a nap in the chapel during the concert, is all. He piles the silver for an alibi in case somebody catches him asleep. When you tell him about Joe he puts it for frosting on the cake like the louse he is."

"You know, Nick," said Bittersohn, "that's one explanation that never occurred to me."

"Because you do not know that slob like I do, Max. Anything, anything he would do to get out of an hour's honest work. I" — Nick turned fiercely to Sarah — "am fat but not a slob. And I work. My God, how I work. So Joe Witherspoon dies and Brown is snoring like a pig in the chapel."

"Vieuxchamp says Witherspoon had dizzy spells. Can you corroborate that?"

"Corroborate no. Believe yes. Joe was an old man, he took no care of himself. Up and down, up and down that murderous staircase he had to climb four, five times a day. Too far out he leans, a little vertigo, maybe, and over he goes."

"But why would he be on the balcony? He belonged in the Titian Room."

"My friend, how should I know? During the concert would maybe be not many people on the third floor. Maybe Joe goes to stretch his legs and watch the pretty peacocks, maybe to take a leak in the waterfall because in this crazy palazzo is only one bathroom and that in the basement. You think the guards go all the way up and down every time?"

Bittersohn glanced at Sarah and changed

the subject. "Did you ever hear Witherspoon talk about the big Titian?"

"As much as he ever talked about anything. Lucrece was his sweetheart. Who could blame him? It is like Shelley, forever will he love and she be fat. So he could only look, big deal. At his age to look was probably all he could manage anyway and for this he got paid. Joe was a lucky man."

"Quite a philosopher, aren't you, Nick? See that guard over by the pillar in the courtyard?"

"Sonny they call him. So?"

"He claims Witherspoon had been complaining lately that Lucrece had changed."

"Maxie, how could a painting change? Joe needed new glasses is all. Or maybe glaucoma or cataract, maybe just old age getting soft in the head. Maybe he was lucky he fell."

"Do you think Witherspoon could have become depressed enough to jump?"

"Who knows? What should it matter jumped or fell? Dead is dead. You like to make mysteries, my friend, here is no mystery. Only a tired old man getting at last a chance to rest his feet."

CHAPTER 4

"I suppose you've got to rush home and cook," said Bittersohn as he helped Sarah into the elegant car he'd left parked along the Fenway.

"Nope." Sarah smiled in rapture and leaned her head back against the rich beige leather upholstery. "I'm off the hook tonight. Mrs. Sorpende's doing supper."

"How come?"

"She offered and I jumped at it. One does get tired of slaving over a hot stove."

"After three months?"

"Closer to eight years. I cooked for the family practically all the time I was married to Alexander."

"You still think about him all the time, don't you?" Bittersohn seemed to be having a little trouble fitting the key into the ignition.

"No, not really. One can't, you know. There's always too much happening. Somebody else getting killed, for instance."

"Look, I'm sorry as hell about today."

"But why should you be?" said Sarah. "You couldn't know this was going to happen. Anyway, according to the statistics, half the violent deaths in Massachusetts occur right here in Boston, and I'm a Bostonian born and bred, so what can I expect? Anyway, this one has nothing whatever to do with me, thank goodness. Unless you think Brooks —"

He started the car a bit less smoothly than usual. "I told you my reasons for wanting to see your cousin this evening. I've never lied to you yet, have I? Maybe it would have been smarter of me to meet him somewhere else, though, instead of dragging you into it."

"Why shouldn't you drag me into it? Can't I be treated like a human being for once?"

"What do you mean? Haven't I been — "

"Oh, it's not you. It's been everybody, all my life. To my parents I was a child they weren't really very interested in, something to be housed and fed and educated according to their ideas, not mine. To Aunt Caroline I was a necessary nuisance. Alexander loved me but he wouldn't have married me if he hadn't felt it his duty, and he acted toward me" — she smiled wryly — "well, when a man's bought you your first ice cream cone and your first swanboat ride I suppose he couldn't help having a sort of daddy knows best attitude, could he? To my relatives I'm just another Kelling, to my boarders I'm the landlady, to you I've sometimes wondered if I was an object of pity. This afternoon you treated me like — I suppose I could say a friend, someone you knew well enough to ask a favor of without wondering whether I'm mature enough to handle it. So please don't spoil things by apologizing."

He shrugged. "What can I say? I don't know where you got that object of pity stuff. Nothing could ever have been farther from my mind. Now shall we make polite remarks about the scenery or would you rather stop for a drink somewhere?"

"I'd love a drink. Why don't we park the car and stroll down to the Hampshire House? If it's not too expensive," Sarah added from force of habit.

"Oh, I guess we can swing a scotch or two. Heard from the newlyweds lately?"

They chatted about Sarah's pontifical cousin Adolphus Kelling and his unlikely but so far blissful marriage to a retired department store saleslady who had been running a one-woman recycling program out

46

of the trash barrels on Boston Common. They left the car in the vast concrete cavern under that same Common and walked down Beacon Street to the rather luxurious restaurant where Bittersohn had bought Sarah lunch on a day she would never forget. She wondered if he remembered, but wouldn't have dreamed of asking after her unexpected burst of self-revelation.

It was late for the early diners and early for the late ones, so they had the cocktail lounge more or less to themselves when they went in. The waitress was content to let them dawdle over their drinks. Sarah was enjoying herself until she happened to catch a glimpse of Bittersohn's watch.

"I really ought to be getting back. Mrs. Sorpende would be dreadfully hurt if I didn't show up on time."

"Okay, you be the landlady and I'll be the boarder." Bittersohn dealt with the check and they walked up the hill to Tulip Street. They were in the nick of time. Cousin Brooks and his lady friend entered the vestibule just as Sarah and her escort were being formally admitted by Charles.

Cousin Brooks had clearly spared no effort to do Sarah proud in front of the household he'd never met before. His sparse gray hair was slicked to pussycat perfection. His aged gray and green tweed suit was pressed until you could cut yourself on the creases. A tailfeather of the crested grebe was stuck into the band of the straw boater he wore to Harvard alumni gatherings.

Dolores Tawne looked exactly as Sarah had pictured her: middle-aged, barrel-shaped, red-faced, red-haired, and belligerently good-humored, pleased at her unexpected treat but ready to squawk if it didn't come up to expectations. She had on a sensible beige tweed coat, a sensible drip-dry beige shirt-waist dress, and sensible brown leather walking shoes. Her gloves were beige nylon, her purse hand-tooled cowhide. A good deal of hand-enameled copper jewelry clanked on wrists and bosom. She was delighted to be there and said so even before Brooks could get her introduced.

"And we're delighted to have you," Sarah replied as needs she must. "Shall we go in and meet the others? Brooks?"

"What? Oh yes," he replied without taking his eyes from a spot above and to the left of Sarah's head. The attraction was, of course, their hostess of the evening, Mrs. Theonia Sorpende.

A while back, Sarah had given Mrs.

Sorpende an armload of lingerie that had been part of her mother-in-law's trousseau back when Georgette and crepe de chine were all the rage and everything was trimmed with six inches of expensive French lace. Out of the chemises, negligees, robes de nuit, and even the step-ins, Mrs. Sorpende had since been creating herself a wardrobe that would have made Mother Machree look like Theda Bara. Tonight since they weren't supposed to be dressing she'd put on what Sarah's grandmother would perhaps have called a tea gown.

Theonia Sorpende was built along the general lines of the Venus de Milo except that she came equipped with soft white arms and exquisitely tapered hands and was more abundantly endowed around the bustline. Her age was a secret hidden behind a Gioconda smile. Her hair had once been raven but was now developing deep auburn highlights where uncharitable persons might assume silver threads would otherwise be starting to show. What she knew about cosmetics was nobody's business. In clinging mauve Georgette and deep flounces of ecru lace she bore a subtle resemblance to Joe Witherspoon's Lucrece, in a fresher, warmer, and even more opulently sexy way.

Luckily Dolores Tawne's skin must be as

thick as her ankles. Quite unaware that she'd just been jilted, she greeted the ageless beauty with cheerful barks and failed to observe how long Mrs. Sorpende's rose-tipped fingers remained clasped in those of Brooks Kelling. Sarah noticed, though, and thought she'd better divert Mrs. Tawne's attention just in case.

"Cousin Brooks tells me you're tremendously clever about taking care of Madam Wilkins's paintings."

That, oddly enough, struck a sore spot. "I'm a painter myself," snapped Dolores. "Didn't Brooks tell you that?"

"Why, I do believe he — "

"I've done the portraits of many prominent people. All the presidents of Amalgamated Enterprises from the founder right down to the present chairman of the board. Six generations."

"My goodness! But surely you couldn't have known them all?"

"No, I'm not that old even if I do look it." Mrs. Tawne slapped a beefy thigh at her own wit. "I work from photographs, of course."

"Oh, I see. It must be extremely difficult."

"Easier than live models. Photographs don't wiggle around." Mrs. Tawne thought that was pretty funny, too. "I always work from photographs."

No doubt Mrs. Tawne had her failings like other mortals but it became clear that excessive modesty was not among them. As they moved into the library for the preprandial sherry that was an invariable part of Sarah's household routine, Dolores held forth on the things she knew how to do, the things she had in fact done, and the heights she might have reached were it not for professional jealousy and backbiting.

During her recital boarders began drifting in: Mr. Eugene Porter-Smith in a navy blue suit with pinstripes and a lemon yellow shirt and tie; Jennifer LaValliere in nothing to speak of; Professor Ormsby in a new green turtleneck jersey that looked much like his old green turtleneck jersey; Mrs. Gates, the new inhabitant of the downstairs suite that was once the drawing room. Mrs. Gates had on a beautifully styled sheer wool dress of a delicate coral that brought out the pink in her cheeks and constrasted charmingly with her silver-white hair.

As it happened, Mrs. Gates had once sat with Mrs. Tawne on a committee for an art exhibition to benefit Children's Hospital. The two began renewing old acquaintance.

Sarah eased herself away from them, wondering where Mr. Bittersohn had got to all of a sudden.

Mariposa, Sarah's confidante, general manager, and comrade, who also posed as the upstairs maid, had the day off to spend with her innumerable relatives. Charles, Mariposa's mentor, roommate, and various other things, was passing around the sherry and hors d'oeuvres. As he offered a silver tray to Sarah, she murmured, "Where did Mr. Bittersohn go? He particularly asked me to invite Mr. Brooks and Mrs. Tawne."

"He is talking on the telephone to London, madam. Scotland Yard have been attempting to reach him for the past several hours."

"Good heavens! I hope he thought to reverse the charges."

Charles gave her the merest flicker of a pitying smile and moved on with his tray. Shortly afterward Mr. Bittersohn rejoined the company, looking more like an advertisement out of *Fortune* magazine than someone who had connections at Scotland yard. Charles threw open the dining room doors and the company flocked in. As was the custom on Sunday nights, supper was set out in massive silver dishes on the buffet and the gentlemen helped the ladies, all but Professor Ormsby, who was much too preoccupied with helping himself.

Mrs. Sorpende had done them proud. Sarah hadn't the faintest idea what she'd prepared, but it all looked delicious. Brooks was gallantly shoveling food on Mrs. Sorpende's own plate. His eyes were level with her magnificent lace-edged décolletage and he was obviously enjoying the view. Fortunately Max Bittersohn had set himself to bowling over Mrs. Tawne, so she was too beguiled to notice her escort's defection. Charles was being attentive to Mrs. Gates, Mr. Porter-Smith to Miss LaValliere. Sarah shrugged and helped herself.

Mrs. Sorpende was indeed a marvelous cook. They went through the buffet like a horde of locusts, then Charles cleared away the plates and brought in a many-layered torte flavored with chocolate, rum, and goodness only knew what else. They had their coffee with the dessert. As appetites grew sated, conversation became more brisk and general. Mrs. Tawne started laying down the law about what was wrong with modern art, which appeared to be a great deal. Young Porter-Smith, a gentleman of unconfined erudition and waspish nature, took exception. Mr. Bittersohn egged them on. Cousin Brooks ignored them and told Mrs. Sorpende all about the snowy egret. She smiled her Mona Lisa smile and made appropriate responses in a voice Sarah heard Brooks comparing favorably to that of the white-winged dove, or *Zenaida asiatica.*

Miss LaValliere, who was a well-brought-up child despite her clothes or lack of them, listened politely to whichever of her elders happened to be talking the loudest at any given moment. Mrs. Gates sipped her tea since she wasn't allowed coffee at night and poured oil on the troubled waters. Professor Ormsby had another large helping of torte.

At last Mr. Bittersohn managed to work the conversation around to the paintings at Madam Wilkins's palazzo. "Mrs. Tawne, what's your opinion of that Romney hanging near the staircase in the Grant Salon?"

"Academic tripe," sneered Mr. Porter-Smith, who hadn't been asked. "Terrible color, tasteless design, lifeless brushwork — "

"It was my opinion the gentleman requested," blazed Mrs. Tawne, "and for your information" — she leaned heavily on every word — "I consider that Romney one of the finest pieces in the entire collection. It represents the art of portraiture raised to an ultimate peak of grace and refinement. Romney's poetic imagery in representing the sitter as Venus with roses and cupids — "

"Theatrical poppycock! The subject was fifty-seven years old when she began posing."

"Fifty-six, and so what? Venus herself would have been a darn sight older than that, wouldn't she?"

"Ah, but Venus was immortal," said Cousin Brooks with a languishing glance at Mrs. Sorpende.

"*Was* immortal is a contradiction in terms." As a certified public accountant, Mr. Porter-Smith did not like getting caught out in an arithmetical error.

"My reason for asking the question, Mrs. Tawne," Bittersohn said loudly enough to be heard above the dissension, "is that it's been suggested to me by someone whose opinion I value highly that the Romney at the Wilkins may possibly be a copy. What is your feeling about that?"

"I thought you were supposed to be the art expert," said Miss LaValliere, who had expended a great deal of effort on Mr. Bittersohn, got absolutely nowhere, and was inclined to nip at his heels as a result.

"Oh, are you?" Mrs. Tawne elevated her sandy eyebrows into the corrugations of her freckled forehead. "Then if an expert like you can't tell, what difference does it make?"

Miss LaValliere giggled most unkindly. Mr. Porter-Smith decided to keep mum and look superior. Sarah thought it was high time to get off Romney.

"Where is your studio, Mrs. Tawne?" she asked. "Do you work right in the museum?"

"No, I've lived at the Fenway Studios for going on forty years now. Be there until I die, I suppose, unless they tear it down."

"Do you know I'm a professional illustrator of sorts myself, but I've never set foot inside a genuine fine artist's studio in my life," Sarah gushed. "I'd adore to see yours sometime."

There wasn't much Mrs. Tawne could say to that but, "You'd be quite welcome any time."

"Then could I possibly come tomorrow, or am I being too pushy? It's just that I happen to have an errand over your way and it's always such a project for me to get away from the house that I try to bunch things together as much as I can. If you're not going to be tied up at the museum, perhaps I could run in for a quick peek."

"When would you be coming?"

"I could manage any time to suit you

between ten and four."

They settled on three o'clock for early tea. Mr. Bittersohn surprised Sarah very much by giving her a surreptitious pat on her neat little derrière behind their chairs before he asked, "Kelling, have you learned anything more about the Witherspoon incident?"

"Only that they managed to get hold of Mr. Fitzroy to tell him and he thinks it's very odd."

"Fitzroy is an old woman," snorted Dolores Tawne, dropping lumps of sugar one after another into her third cup of coffee.

"Now, Dolores," said Brooks, "don't be unfair just because you and he don't always see eye to eye. Mr. Fitzroy is an extremely able administrator."

"Oh, is he?" She sipped her sirupy stimulant with sibylline susurrations. "I could tell you a few things."

"Such as what, Mrs. Tawne?" Bittersohn asked.

"Just shop. It wouldn't interest an expert like you."

"Well." Cousin Brooks ruffled his feathers like a perky old Bewick's wren. "I'll soon have a chance to pass on the inside information to you, Bittersohn. Mr. Fitzroy has asked me to fill Joe's place until the trustees can select a new guard."

Dolores turned a shade redder than she'd already been. "Is that so? He might have had the common decency to consult with me first."

"But it's been you who've suggested me as a substitute for your own brother on any number of occasions," Brooks expostulated. "Otherwise Mr. Fitzroy would never have thought of me, I'm sure."

"I'm not saying you won't do an adequate job, Brooks. It's just his high-handed way of doing things that gets my goat."

"I hadn't realized you were on the board of trustees, Mrs. Tawne," remarked Mrs. Gates.

"I'm not, exactly," Dolores admitted, "but I'm proud to say that for over a quarter of a century I have enjoyed the complete confidence of Mr. Palmerston."

"There was a Mr. Palmerston who used to come to the house sometimes when Aunt Caroline and Leila Lackridge were involved in the Arts Festival," said Sarah. "Is this the same man, I wonder? C. Edwald Palmerston. I never did know what the C was for."

"Cadwallader," said Mr. Porter-Smith, who always knew things like that.

"Exactly." Mrs. Tawne nodded as though she'd scored a point, although Sarah couldn't imagine why. "Mr. Palmerston has been chairman of our board of trustees for over thirty years. He relies on me to keep him informed about the day-to-day affairs at the museum."

"Mr. Palmerston seems to be on a great many boards," Mrs. Gates observed.

"He is. I've never known anyone with a deeper sense of civic responsibility."

Interfering old coot was what Cousin Dolph called him, Sarah recalled. At least that was the politest thing she could recall. To be fair, however, the same things had probably been said about Dolph before the former Miss Mary Smith took him in hand.

"I wonder what Palmerston will have to say about the attempted robbery," said Bittersohn innocently.

Dolores Tawne pounced. "Robbery? What robbery? I didn't hear about any robbery. Brooks, why didn't you tell me? What happened?"

"Nothing. Sarah here found Brown, the adipose sacristan of the chapel, wedged under a pew. The silver had been taken from the altar and heaped on the floor. Brown told a tale of being slugged by some would-be thieves who, he claimed, must have shoved Witherspoon off the balcony to keep him from identifying them. It's a lot of balderdash, of course."

"Well, of all the — I never heard — wait till I — "

Sarah quickly poured Mrs. Tawne another cup of coffee and watched with anxiety while she gulped it down. The woman was an alarming color now.

"Mrs. Tawne, you mustn't let your work upset you so."

"Upset me? Why, that idiot!" The artist fought herself under control, gradually fading to a less apoplectic shade of red. "Pulling a ridiculous schoolboy trick like that while poor old Joe was lying dead in the garden. Robbers my foot! Joe lost his balance and fell, that was all. I'm not surprised. I've caught my own brother Jimmy more than once hanging over that slippery balustrade to look at the clock, and bawled him out for it good and proper I can tell you. Don't let me catch you doing such a thing, Brooks."

"I'm no clock watcher," said Kelling stiffly, "and neither was Witherspoon."

"I didn't say Joe was watching the clock," she huffed. "I said he was looking at it. I only wish it had been that imbecile Brown."

Mrs. Sorpende, with her ineffable tact, channeled the talk into a more refined vein. "You are both highly privileged to be entrusted with the protection and preservation of priceless art treasures," she cooed.

"I feel the responsibility keenly," Brooks assured her.

Mrs. Sorpende arranged the fall of lace over a plump and comely wrist. "One feels that Mr. Fitzroy must be a penetrating judge of character."

Cousin Brooks edged still closer to the billows of mauve Georgette. Dolores Tawne finally realized what was happening.

"Well, I've got to be getting along," she snapped. "Early to bed for us working gals. Thanks for the supper, Mrs. Kelling. You coming, Brooks?"

It was a struggle, but the Code of the Kellings prevailed. Sarah rewarded Brooks for good behavior by expressing a cordial wish that he wouldn't be such a stranger. Mrs. Sorpende added an intimation that she was always at home in the evenings. Brooks gave his word of honor that he would indeed not be such a stranger and nobody present doubted his sincerity.

"It was so nice you could come, Mrs. Tawne," said Sarah. "Then I'll see you tomorrow at three."

"What? Oh yes. Tomorrow at three."

Dolores and Brooks both looked rather downcast as they left, though no doubt for different reasons.

CHAPTER 5

"Personally," said Sarah, "I found the salt of the earth a trifle on the peppery side."

She was doing the dishes, having complimented Mrs. Sorpende fulsomely on the truly delectable meal and shooed her off to be gracious to Professor Ormsby in the library. Mariposa wasn't back from her relatives' yet. Charles was down in the basement playing Bach on the stereo, for Charles was a young man of highbrow tastes. Max Bittersohn was ostensibly in his own basement quarters but had in fact lingered to dry the dishes for Sarah.

"A highly combustible lady," he agreed. "I wonder why she went into fits when I told her about Brown."

"Perhaps she felt any burglar should ask her permission before slugging a guard, though I got the impression she didn't believe his yarn any more than you did."

"No, she must know her Brown better

than she does her Romneys. Unless she's well aware the painting is a fake and won't admit it for fear of undermining the museum's prestige. How come your family hasn't pointed out that little discrepancy ages ago?"

"The Kellings and the Madam didn't get along." Sarah told him about the fiasco at the opening. "So if anybody had said anything after that, it would have been taken for another piece of cattiness. Anyway, none of us ever went back. Except for Brooks I expect I'm the first Kelling to have set foot in the place since that opening soiree. And Brooks wouldn't know about the Romney because his mother had a fight with Aunt Emma about Rudy Vallee back around 1928 and they never spoke after that, so naturally he's never visited Aunt Emma. Anyway, she probably wouldn't have asked him because Brooks is looked upon as a bit of a renegade."

"I wondered what a Kelling was doing giving bird calls at kids' birthday parties."

"Laying them in the aisles, I don't doubt. Brooks can be great fun, especially with children. He's the original rolling stone, though I expect he's fairly mossy as far as money goes. His father cut him off without a penny when he refused to go into the family wool business after college, but Brooks had a little trust fund from some great-aunt or somewhere. Kellings are always inheriting odd bits from here and there. Anyway, Brooks's father died of apoplexy the day Roosevelt got nominated for a fourth term and his widow decided to become a female tycoon. She ran the business into the ground in about six months and skipped off to Zurich with whatever she could salvage before the receivers moved in, so it was a stroke of luck for Brooks that he'd been written off the books. Otherwise he'd have been stuck for whatever he had, I suppose. As it is, Brooks has managed to live more or less as he pleases. I've always been sorry not to see more of him, but my own father held it against Brooks that he didn't step in and rescue his father's firm and I think Dolph still does, though in fact Brooks couldn't have done a thing. His mother must have been another Dolores Tawne from what I've heard about her. Maybe that's why he keeps getting himself involved with female bullies. Anyway, Brooks never liked Aunt Caroline and I'm afraid he thought Alexander rather spineless, though he used to show up once in a while collecting funds to build homes for indigent bluebirds and so forth. I have a hunch Brooks didn't come to see me after Alexander died because he was out of town at the time and didn't see the papers, so he's been under the impression I was left a rich widow. Now that he knows I'm flat broke, he'll no doubt be camping on the doorstep offering to put on the screens and fix the dripping faucets."

"So let him. Where's he living now?"

"I forgot to ask. Some rooming house, I expect. He moves a lot. His landladies are always indigent widows like me and he gets to suspecting they have designs on him, which I'm sure they do."

"I hope he doesn't move on till I get him to find out whether Joe Witherspoon had his fly zipped when he fell."

"Why, Mr. Bittersohn, you do bring up the most thought-provoking subjects of conversation."

"I thought you wanted to be one of the gang."

"I do, honestly, and I see exactly what you're getting at. So you intend to pursue this affair at the Madam's even though you haven't been engaged or commissioned or whatever the term is?"

"Try hired. Sure, why not? The trustees can't put me on the case till they know they've got troubles, can they? I'm like those lawyers who chase ambulances. They never know if they're going to get a bloody nose or a nice, juicy insurance settlement out of it, but they give it the old school try just in case. Where do these cups go?"

"Leave them on the counter. We'll want them for breakfast. Oh, dear, there's the doorbell. I'd better go."

But Charles was already leaping up the basement stairs, snapping on his pre-fabricated tie and buttoning his coat en route. By the time he got to the door he was Mr. Hudson personified. A moment later he was back in the kitchen, stiff as a Celluloid collar. "A Mr. Fieringer to see Mr. Bittersohn and – er – his beautiful lady friend."

"I expect he means me," said Sarah, blushing slightly. "Mr. Bittersohn and I were at Mr. Fieringer's concert this afternoon. How did he know where to find us, I wonder, if he couldn't even remember my name?"

"Asked somebody," said Bittersohn. "I told you Nick knows everybody."

"I wonder what he wants. Charles, are

67

Mrs. Sorpende and the others still in the library?"

"Yes, madam."

"Then you'd better show Mr. Fieringer up to the studio. Take him a liqueur if he wants one and tell him we'll be right along."

Sarah had planned to use Aunt Caroline's former boudoir on the second floor as a workroom. However, she'd soon found that she required a private sitting room since Mrs. Gates was now sleeping in the drawing room and the boarders were using the library as a common room, and she couldn't very well hold tête-à-têtes in her own bedroom without giving rise to comment.

Mary and Dolph had contributed two charming bergères and a love seat out of Great-uncle Frederick's overstuffed mansion in Chestnut Hill, where they now lived. Anora Protheroe had given a Tiffany lamp and, rather touchingly, Charlotte Hunnewell Lamson's charming conté crayon portrait of Anora herself as a younger and far hand-somer woman. A grateful client had given Max Bittersohn one of Philip Hale's Beacon Hill tea parties and he'd passed the painting on to Sarah, saying it was more her type of thing than his, which was certainly true, so she couldn't have refused it if she'd cared to and needless to say she didn't. Sarah's drawing table stood over under the window. Her supplies, favorite books, and a few treasures were neatly housed in white-painted cabinets and shelves Mariposa's cousin the carpenter had built and Mariposa's cousin the painter had finished in white enamel. It was now as dainty a sitting room as any lady could wish and the impresario looked grossly out of place in it.

As the two entered he bounced to his feet. "I hope I'm not interrupting something." He made it sound like a dirty joke.

"Not at all," said Sarah. "My butler gave me to understand that you wished to see both Mr. Bittersohn and myself. Otherwise he would have shown you to Mr. Bittersohn's own quarters. Downstairs," she added with enough emphasis to make Bittersohn's lips twitch. "If you prefer to talk privately with him, I'll excuse myself."

"Who would deprive himself of the company of so beautiful a lady? Eh, Bittersohn?"

"What's on your mind, Nick?" Bittersohn replied testily. "I'm rather tied up just now."

"Maxie, is this kind of you? I stop by to wish good health and long life to my friend and his beautiful lady and I get the bum's rush."

"Sit down and shut up, Nick," sighed Bittersohn. "Mrs. Kelling is my landlady and she'll charge me extra if I notice what she looks like. Oddly enough, though, we were talking about you a while back. Weren't we, Mrs. Kelling?"

Sarah couldn't recall that they had, but she nodded. "Yes, with Mrs. Tawne."

"Mrs. Tawne? You know Dolores?" Fieringer was surprised, and not pleasantly.

"She was here to supper. My cousin brought her."

"So? It's a small world. A wonderful woman, Dolores, the salt of the earth. But thick in the ankles."

"How about the head?" asked Bittersohn.

The fat man blinked. "Not there, no. Dolores is a smart cookie. Very capable woman."

"Why do you say that?"

"Why? How do I know why? The good Lord gave her brains maybe to make up for that face. Is it permitted that I smoke, gracious landlady?"

"The little china dish on the table beside you is an ashtray," Sarah replied, wondering why the impresario was sweating so.

"What does Mrs. Tawne do around the Madam's?" Bittersohn persisted.

"She sticks her fingers in the pies. She dusts the priceless you should excuse the expression art objects. She makes little repairs when everything falls apart in the dampness from that imbecile fountain. She nags her poor halfwit brother into eternal vigilance over the moths in the tapestries when he would rather go and be happy in his spiritual home, Paddy O'Malley's Bar."

"I trust she won't try to make things difficult for Cousin Brooks," said Sarah.

"Brooks? Brooks Kelling? Could he be your cousin you speak of? Little Kelling the framer?"

"Does Brooks do framing? I didn't know that."

"Sure. Tawne paints, Kelling frames. Two hearts that beat as one. Why should Dolores give Kelling a hard time? He isn't around much anyway."

"He will be for a while. He's agreed to fill in for that guard who was killed this afternoon falling from the third floor until the trustees can hire a replacement. Mrs. Tawne acted rather miffed about it."

So, oddly enough, did Fieringer. "Dolores didn't tell me."

"She didn't know herself until Brooks happened to mention it while we were at the table. She was furious because Mr. Fitzroy asked him without consulting her first."

"She would be." Having taken only a couple of nervous puffs, Fieringer stubbed out his cigarette with elaborate care. "Did she have anything to say about Joe?"

"She thinks he fell over the balustrade while he was trying to see the clock and Brown faked the robbery as a bid for attention," Bittersohn answered for Sarah.

"And you, my friend?"

"Me?" Max Bittersohn's gray blue eyes were wide with innocence. "You've got it all figured out, Nick. You told us this afternoon what happened."

"Maxie, don't try to kid old Nick. I know your mind. Somebody dies, Bittersohn says, Who done it?" Fieringer laughed but his eyes were watchful slits in their nests of lard. "Is it not so, gracious landlady?"

"You've known him longer than I have," Sarah said in what she hoped was a noncommittal tone. "Are you closely associated with the Madam's also, Mr. Fieringer?"

"Call me Nick. Everybody calls me Nick. In a way, yes." The impresario lit another cigarette and waved it around like a baton. I organize all the concerts at a stipend that pays for my bad habit of smoking but lucky for me they give the matches free thrown in at the time of purchase. The concerts give me anyway opportunity to expose my fine young artists before the discerning public. Tell me honest, Max, you think the cellist has promise?"

"The kid's going to be okay, Nick. Give her another year." By which time, his shrug implied, she might with luck have taken up the kazoo instead of the cello. "How well do you know C. Edwald Palmerston?"

"See, I told you." Nick Fieringer turned to Sarah, flinging his arms wide and almost burning a hole with his cigarette in the new curtains she'd scrimped for out of her housekeeping budget. "Already he's investigating. Never mind is there anything to investigate, Bittersohn investigates. Max, my friend, I confess all. It was Fitzroy pushed Joe because Joe makes weewee in the fountain. How does Fitzy manage when on Sunday he teaches Bible lessons to forty little angel boys? You tell me, my friend. You're the detective."

"I asked you a question," said Bittersohn.

Nick threw up his pudgy hands. "All right, I did it! I killed Joe because he had a tin ear. Or maybe Bernie did it because Joe drank up his rubbing alcohol on him. Or maybe Dolores Tawne is right and Joe fell and Max Bittersohn should investigate how beautiful is his landlady who has known him so short a time and might like to know him better, eh? Lay off, my friend. Here are only a few old guards and one fat impresario trying to make a lousy living."

"Sure, Nick, sure. How about stepping down to Charles Street for a drink?"

"I could have something sent up here," Sarah offered, but Fieringer refused.

"Thank you no. I have to go tell my little cellist the great Max Bittersohn says she's a genius she should maybe start looking for a rich husband. I have to find Bernie and make him eat something so he won't get DT's until after Wednesday's concert. And tomorrow at half-past seven in the morning I audition a tuba player. My God, what a life!"

He kissed Sarah's hand all the way up to the elbow, pounded Bittersohn shatteringly between the shoulder blades, and waddled off.

"I wonder," mused Bittersohn, "why he never answered my question about C. Edwald Palmerston?"

CHAPTER 6

Punctually at three o'clock Monday afternoon, Sarah Kelling tapped on Dolores Tawne's door in that wonderful anachronism, the Fenway Studios. Dolores greeted the guest effusively enough to make it clear she wasn't really welcome and made a great fuss of getting her seated.

Sarah had found the outside of the building exciting architecturally and well worth the efforts being made to preserve it for its original purpose. Except for the little balcony and the flight of stairs that led down to the floor, Dolores's studio was something of a letdown: merely a large, squarish room unusual only in being about a story and a half high with enormously long windows. A half-finished still life of vegetables and a dead pheasant was set ostentatiously on a heavy easel. The place reeked of turpentine.

Feeling a bit queasy from the smell, Sarah

remarked that the painting looked as if it would be quite lovely when it was finished. Mrs. Tawne agreed, pointing out the more potentially delightful spots with a mahlstick. Sarah asked if Mrs. Tawne had other works in progress at the moment and Mrs. Tawne said no she hadn't. Sarah said she herself worked mostly in pen and ink and it must be fun to handle color. Mrs. Tawne gave Sarah a lecture on color theory that Sarah had learned when she was twelve. Then she presented Sarah with a little scrapbook to look at while she made the tea.

None of the clippings was very recent. Most of them dealt at what Sarah found to be unnecessary length with the centennial celebration of a corporation for which Dolores Agnew Tawne, prominent Boston artist, had painted a series of presidential portraits. There was a blurry photograph of Dolores having her hand shaken by a prognathous executive in front of a regrettably exact likeness of himself. There were photographs of the other portraits. To Sarah, brought up among works of art, they showed technical competence and no spark of genuine creativity.

She was conscientiously trying to interest herself in the history of Amalgamated Enterprises when her hostess came back from the small inner area that must serve as bedroom and kitchen staggering under the weight of an overloaded tea tray.

"I can still enjoy my food, thank the Lord," Mrs. Tawne remarked as she set down the tray. "Try a sandwich. That's egg salad and here's deviled ham and" – her recital of the menu was interrupted by a loud knocking on the door – "and there's my star boarder, no doubt. I swear she could smell food all the way from Kenmore Square. Excuse me."

She bounded up the stairs and flung open the door. "Why, Mr. Palmerston!"

C. Edwald Palmerston, for it was none other as Sarah noted to her consternation, removed the pearl-gray fedora that had been set with geometric precision across his balding head. "Good afternoon, Mrs. Tawne. I happened to be in the neighborhood on a matter of business and took the liberty of dropping by. There are some important matters on which I should greatly appreciate the benefit of your opinion. Might you have a moment to spare for me?"

Sarah ate a sardine sandwich and mentally cursed her luck. Mrs. Tawne came as close to fluttering as her utilitarian contours permitted.

"Mr. Palmerston, you know I always have time for you. Let me take your hat. Come right down and join us for tea. I believe you're acquainted with Mrs. Kelling?"

"Kelling? Why, I – "

Sarah fought down an impulse to scream and said politely, "How do you do, Mr. Palmerston? We met at Mrs. Lackridge's and you also came to our house when you served on the festival committee with her and my mother-in-law."

"Ah, yes. Yes indeed. This is an unexpected pleasure, Mrs. – ah – Kelling."

Judging from C. Edwald's expression it was a pleasure he could have done nicely without. The late Caroline Kelling, though both deaf and blind, had been far from dumb in any sense of the word. She had called Mr. Palmerston a hare-brained old fool in open meeting and proven her case. Sarah had been present on that occasion and Mr. Palmerston must have remembered. The silence became strained.

Dolores, however, was not the girl to let a party die. She bustled back and forth plying her guests with food and drink, twitching the gauze curtains over the huge studio windows to shield Mr. Palmerston's august eyeballs from the outside glare, chattering without a break. Just as she'd got everything and everybody arranged to her own satisfaction and plumped herself down with a cup and plate, another visitor knocked.

"There she is now," she sighed. "What a bother. Excuse me, folks. I'll try to put her off."

Mrs. Tawne did not succeed. When she came back downstairs she was closely followed by the much bedizened wreck of a woman who must once have been quite breathtaking.

"This is my neighbor, Countess Ouspenska, Mrs. Kelling. Have you met the countess, Mr. Palmerston?"

The countess gave Sarah an absentminded glance, then turned the full glare of her eye shadow on Palmerston. "You do not see me."

"I – er – see you quite plainly. That is, I – er – in fact, it has been some time since – er – would you care to sit down?"

Looking even more foolish than he had on that historic day when Aunt Caroline put him through the wringer, Mr. Palmerston straightened his lanky frame and went through the motions of offering Countess Ouspenska his chair.

She spurned him and took Dolores's instead. "I sit here. Who is this pretty little girl you make a fool of yourself over now?"

After a dazed moment, Sarah realized the countess was talking about her. "I came by myself," she said firmly.

"This is Mrs. Alexander Kelling, Brooks Kelling's cousin," snapped their hostess.

"Kelling? But that is the name of the woman who murders everybody and lives with the beautiful Max! Can it be? Ah, yes, I see it can be! There is excitement in your face. Adventure! Passion!" She bit hugely into an egg salad sandwich. "Naturally a *grande amoureuse* like you would not bother with an old poop like this Palmerston. Tell me confidentially as one adventuress to another, how do you get away with it?"

Sarah didn't know whether to laugh or flee. "First, I wish you'd understand that I've never murdered anybody. Second, if you're referring to Mr. Max Bittersohn, I don't live with him. He lives with me. That is" — she felt her face getting hot — "I have a boarding house and he happens to be one of my boarders. There's very little adventure involved in being a landlady, I assure you."

"Ho! Never mind, little one. If I could get the magnificent Max to live with me I would keep my secrets also. It is so beautiful and so sad."

"Why is it sad?"

"Because he chooses you and not me. All joy is sadness. That is life. I will have more of your good tea, Dolores, and many of these amusing little cakes. Then I will take this so demure little seductress to my studio and we will talk of love and Max Bittersohn."

"That's a splendid idea," said Mrs. Tawne briskly. "Will you have another cup of tea before you go, Mrs. Kelling?"

Sarah thought she might as well because she couldn't resist the countess's invitation and it didn't look as though they'd be leaving for some time yet from the way the woman was tucking into the refreshments. At last, however, the point of satiety appeared to have been reached. Countess Ouspenska wiped her lips on the fancy paper napkin Dolores had supplied, carefully wrapped the few remaining sandwiches in it, and announced, "We go."

Sarah picked up her handbag, thanked Mrs. Tawne for a delightful visit — it had been an unusual one, at any rate — and followed her exotic new acquaintance down the hall. Countess Ouspenska's studio was similar in architecture to the one they'd just left but totally different otherwise. Dolores Tawne's had been antiseptically neat, this was an exuberant welter. There was a great deal of furniture, none of it any good, all of it in desperate need of dusting. There were tapestry runners and vases of paper flowers. There must have been at least a dozen icons sitting about and to Sarah's astonishment these looked like the real thing.

The countess set the packet of sandwiches with care on the shelf of a broken-down Chinese étagère. "Dolores is dull but kind of heart," she observed. "This week for me is rent so not food."

Sarah blinked. She'd thought she herself was hard up, but so far she'd never had to miss a meal. "Surely those icons," she stammered, "they look as though they're valuable. Couldn't you – ?"

"Sell? Not. Never. Without my icons I starve in the gutter," said the countess cheerfully. "Look what I do."

She led her guest through the maze of furniture to a table on which sat one of the icons. Beside it, in a litter of twisted paint tubes, whiskered brushes, and wads of filthy cotton, lay an absolute duplicate complete except for the gold leaf on the Infant's halo.

"I finish tomorrow. Is most careful work to make identical in every detail. I sell, then I eat. If I could paint faster I could eat more. Is always market for beautiful fake icons and nobody can fake as good as me. I am unique."

"I'm sure you are," said Sarah, and hoped it was true. "Where do you sell them?"

"Ah, that is my secret. Never with ten thousand tortures will I tell. Is no good for business, see?"

"Of course, I should have known better than to ask. I beg your pardon."

"I am wonderful businesswoman," said the countess with a complacency that her circumstances would not appear to justify. "Is necessary now that I am old and ugly."

"Oh, you're not!"

"Pretty words from a pretty woman is nice but I say the hell with women's lib give me every time a man to pay the bills. For you the wonderful Max coughs up, eh?"

"He pays his rent like the rest of my boarders," Sarah replied primly. "I was left badly off when my husband was killed. It was a case of either losing my house or finding a way to make it produce some income, so I started to rent rooms. As to the murders, Mr. Bittersohn was very helpful with the investigation."

"And now he investigates you, eh? Ah, if I were twenty years younger maybe I could have been investigated by the gorgeous Max instead of that old turkey who sits and gobbles with Dolores."

"But surely you don't mean — he couldn't possibly — "

"Mr. Watch-and-Ward Palmerston? Not any more he couldn't I think but he would no doubt still wish to. I knew him long ago, when he was somewhat less unattractive than now. He was, I will say for him, a man who always got his money's worth. So I have heard from a number of sources. I meet ladies in all walks of life, some of whom are in fact not what you would call ladies and do more walking than others, if you follow me as he does not nowadays. He is a philosopher. He took them where he found them and he paid them what they asked. About the price he never quibbled, only about what a big financier calls the return on the dollar."

"If my Great-aunt Matilda had ever known that! She was always holding him up to my Cousin Dolph as a model."

"Palmerston was never that good," said Countess Ouspenska. "Now, if it would be the handsome and agile Max, tell me — "

Anticipating what the countess was hoping to hear, Sarah jumped up. "I'm afraid all I can tell you is that if I'm not home in time

84

to prepare Mr. Bittersohn's dinner he might employ his agility in moving elsewhere. Thank you so much for showing me your studio."

"Come again after I sell my icon and I give you tea Russian style. Bring your marvelous Max." The countess kissed her repeatedly on both cheeks.

"I'm sure he'd love to come." Sarah decided it was no use trying again to explain that the marvelous Max wasn't hers to bring. She had periodic fits of the giggles all the way back to Tulip Street. En route she stopped at one of the more chichi grocery stores and ordered a basket of exotic delicacies to be sent to the Countess Ouspenska at the Fenway Studios, charging it to Mrs. Adolphus Kelling because she couldn't possibly pay for the basket herself and she knew Cousin Mary would understand.

"We'll send it around first thing in the morning, Mrs. Kelling," the clerk promised. "Did you wish to enclose a card?"

"Why not?" Sarah picked up the pen he offered, thought a moment, then printed, "In fond remembrance," on the little white square and sealed it inside the envelope. At least the countess would eat this week.

CHAPTER 7

The magnificent Max did not appear for the dinner Sarah cooked. He finally showed up about half-past nine while she was in the library exchanging recipes with Mrs. Sorpende. She could see that he looked frazzled around the edges.

"Mr. Bittersohn, did you have any dinner? Shall I fix you a snack?"

"That would be great. I'm starved." He followed Sarah out to the kitchen. Mrs. Sorpende, being an oracle by trade and perhaps divining that her *persona* might be *non grata* there, did not.

Mariposa and Charles were in their basement lair broadening their cultural horizons by listening to some old Cab Calloway records. Sarah shut the basement door on Minnie the Moocher and sat Bittersohn down at the table with a cup of soup for starters. "Now tell me what's happened."

"Brown, that guard who staged the robbery in the chapel — "

"I know. Drink your soup while it's hot."

"Brooks found him dead in the locker room this afternoon full of paint remover. He had a note in his pocket saying 'I'm sorry about Joe.'"

"Oh no!"

"Lieutenant Davies can't decide whether Brown killed Witherspoon and then committed suicide in a fit of remorse or got thirsty while he was trying to write somebody a sympathy letter."

"What do you think?"

"I think the note was a plant. I think Brown kept a bottle in his locker and somebody loaded it. After he passed out they took away the liquor bottle and substituted one half full of paint remover with the label nice and prominent and his fingerprints artistically arranged on the glass. Very efficient job. Also a very painful way to go, one might think. It must have taken him a while to die, unless the paint remover was gingered up with a pinch of strychnine or something."

"Are they going to do an autopsy?"

"Have to, I suppose. How did your visit with Mrs. Tawne go?"

Sarah could readily understand why he'd

want to change the subject. "It was interesting, in a way," she told him. "C. Edwald Palmerston dropped in unexpectedly. Mrs. Tawne seemed ever so glad to see him. And I met an admirer of yours."

"Do tell. Which one?"

"Countess Ouspenska, no less."

"Ouspenska?" He took another spoonful of soup. "What does she look like?"

"In a word, hell. Slavic and suffering. I'd say, though, that she must have been absolutely stunning when she was a good deal younger and in better repair."

"Oh, I know who you mean now. Good old Lydia. She used to be Nick Fieringer's girl."

"She was C. Edwald Palmerston's girl, too."

"Small world. Does Mrs. Tawne know that?"

"I couldn't say. The countess greeted him like an old acquaintance against whom she held a grudge, but she didn't unburden her soul, as it were, until she and I had gone to her studio. And then she talked mostly about you."

"What's to unburden about me? My God, Mrs. Kelling, you don't imagine Lydia and I were ever — "

"No, I don't. That was the burden of her plaint. That you hadn't, I mean. She" – Sarah blushed – "appeared to be under some misapprehension as to – "

Luckily Charles poked his head into the kitchen just then. "Oh, Mr. Bittersohn. I heard movement overhead and thought that might be you fixing yourself a snack since you weren't in to dinner. I was about to offer my assistance but I see you are capably provided for. May I fetch you a glass of sherry, perhaps? Or a cold beer? Mariposa and I keep a six-pack or two on hand for our personal use."

"No, thanks, Charlie. I'm sort of off liquor tonight. Just tell me if you happen to know a former actress named Lydia Ouspenska."

Charles carefully shut the basement door, cocked an ear to make sure Mariposa wasn't on her way upstairs, then murmured, "I have met Countess Ouspenska, sir."

"She's madly in love with Mr. Bittersohn," Sarah couldn't resist putting in.

"I have always found her to be a person of unexceptionable taste and discrimination, madam. She comes from a noble Russian family."

"She's a Polish sign painter's daughter from Chelsea," said Bittersohn. "The way I heard it, the Countess Ouspenska act came from a play she was in, back during World War II when all the real actresses were doing their bit for the lads at the front. Lydia never got far in the theater. Her real forte was seeing what the boys in the back room would have. How's she doing these days, Mrs. Kelling?"

"Not too well. All her former sources of income have walked out on her. Charles, how could you be such a cad?"

"Madam, I must beg leave to protest. My connection with Countess Ouspenska has been confined to a short run at the Charles Street Playhouse, where we both had walkons, and since then to an occasional exchange of pleasantries over a libation or two at Irving's."

"I didn't know you hung out in Coolidge Corner, Charlie," said Bittersohn.

"Officially, sir, I do not. However, all Mariposa's relatives live over the other way in Jamaica Plain and environs, and there are times when we theatricals require our freedom of expression. If I can render no further service here, may I return to my quarters?"

"You have our gracious permission to retire. On your way downstairs, you might try to recall whether Lydia's ever said anything to you about Madam Wilkins's palazzo."

"I shall endeavor to do so. *Hasta la vista, señor, señora.*"

"Mariposa's teaching him Spanish though I don't know why she bothers. It looks to me as they conduct most of their conversations in sign language." Sarah laughed and blushed. "I must have spent a little too long with Countess Ouspenska. Getting back to her finances, Mr. Bittersohn, did you know she supports herself these days by manufacturing antique icons?"

"Are they any good?"

"As good as they can be, I should say. She showed me one that was almost finished and I'll bet even you would be hard put to tell the difference between the copy and the original."

"Where did she get the icon she copies from?"

"She owns about a dozen different ones. I couldn't tell whether they were all genuine, of course, but they looked awfully good to me. She said she'd never part with them because they're what keep her from starving in the gutter. But what struck me most was that if she's such a clever forger — "

"Yes, one might wonder, mightn't one? You're thinking about that Romney, I expect, and maybe a few dozen other things. That wouldn't explain Brown and Witherspoon, though, would it? I can't see Lydia ever bumping off a man."

"She'd kill them with kindness, I suppose."

"Why, Mrs. Kelling! For a nice little girl from Beacon Hill you're getting awfully free in your talk all of a sudden."

"It must be the dissolute company I'm keeping. Would you like me to visit Countess Ouspenska again and pump her about the Madam's?"

"No, I want you to stay away from her and also from the palazzo. I'm putting another of my secret agents on the case tomorrow."

"How impressive. Who is he?"

"He prefers to be called Bill Jones. Bill knows every hot painting that's been peddled in and out of Boston for the past thirty years."

"Does he steal them himself, or what?"

"No, he just likes to keep track. One might call it a hobby. Bill's a highly successful commercial artist, as a matter of fact. You'd probably enjoy meeting him."

"Then why don't you bring him to dinner?"

"Maybe I will. What's up now, Charlie? I thought you'd retired to your quarters."

The butler, who had manifested himself in the doorway, stiffened to attention. "Mr. Brooks Kelling has arrived. He wishes to be announced."

"Did Mrs. Tawne come with him?" Sarah asked with a sinking feeling.

"No, madam. He is in the library with Mrs. Sorpende."

"Why, the little dickens! Give him another few minutes' billing and cooing time while Mr. Bittersohn finishes his supper, then show him up to the studio. Was that what you wanted me to say, Mr. Bittersohn?"

"Precisely that." He gobbled the last few bites of food. "Shall we dance?"

As they went up the back stairs it occurred to Sarah to wonder if her other boarders were aware how much time Mr. Bittersohn had been spending in that upstairs sitting room lately, and how the *soi-disant* Countess Ouspenska had got the notion she and he were carrying on what might delicately be described as a close relationship.

Jennifer LaValliere and Eugene Porter-Smith went about together a good deal. Had one of them happened to drop a remark down at one of the coffee houses they frequented that somehow got passed on to her? Or was Sarah getting herself gossiped about more than she realized by appearing in public so often these days with Mr. Bittersohn?

But how could anybody who knew Sarah Kelling also know Lydia Ouspenska? Mr. Palmerston did, for one, but he was barely on speaking terms with Sarah and whatever liaison he'd had with the countess had obviously been over long ago. Dolores Tawne would have had to jump to some awfully swift conclusions since she'd met the pair for the first time Sunday night in what could hardly be called a compromising situation.

Nick Fieringer did. And Nick had been sitting here with them both last night making suggestive remarks about beautiful ladies, and there was no denying the fact that it was a cozy, intimate sort of place and that Sarah's own bedroom happened to be on the other side of a connecting door and perhaps that door hadn't been quite shut. And Nick was supposed to be an old boyfriend of Lydia's. But Nick was old in years, too, and he'd said he had to audition a tuba player at the crack of dawn. Surely he wouldn't have gone dashing over to Ipswich Street last night to inform the countess that Max Bittersohn, with whom she was evidently acquainted mainly by wishful thinking, might or might not be having a little something on with the widow Kelling, whom Lydia had met only that same afternoon.

Of course Nick might have seen Lydia sometime today. And today Brown the guard had died from drinking paint remover, as surely no sane man would do of his own free will. And Lydia Ouspenska was an artist. And paint remover was the sort of thing an artist might think of. And she was also a superb copyist. And what had Brooks found out to bring him tearing over here again tonight?

Maybe it wasn't anything so very urgent at that. Brooks was in no hurry to leave Mrs. Sorpende. Sarah and the magnificent Max had plenty of time to settle themselves in the two bergères and sit until the silence became awkward.

At last Bittersohn remarked, "I like this room."

"It's rather small."

"Maybe that's why it's so pleasant."

He did have a sensitive, curving mouth for a man whose other features had at first looked so rugged in contrast to her late husband's. She tried to picture Alexander's face and found to her secret horror that she could remember him best as a pair of long legs in impeccable gray flannel, taking a little girl to feed the ducks in the Public Gardens. Yet she'd loved Alexander with all her heart. Well, of course not entirely all. She'd loved her parents, she supposed, and she loved Aunt Emma and dear old Anora Protheroe and Uncle Jem and maybe his faithful henchman Egbert a little and she was getting extremely fond of Cousin Mary and even, after all these years, of Cousin Dolph. There had to be many different kinds of loving and hearts couldn't very well be amenable to quantitative analysis. And what on earth was keeping Brooks?

He came curvetting in at last, sleek and lithe as an elderly chipmunk. "Good evening, children."

"Hi, Kelling," said Bittersohn. "Found any more bodies?"

"Not yet, but point me in the right direction and I'll be glad to go hunting. I came for my instructions."

"Nice of you. I don't suppose there's any chance of finding the bottle Brown really drank out of?"

"Naturally I conducted a thorough search of the premises and it's nowhere to be found. That in itself is a telling point, don't you think? I daresay it was tossed out somewhere in the Fens. Another broken whiskey bottle over there would hardly be noticed. I've written to the *Christian Science Monitor* about littering more than once."

"And scholarly epistles they were, no doubt. Why else do you think Brown was murdered?"

"I knew the man, if one could dignify him by that name. Brown was a slug. Slugs don't go around committing painful and melodramatic suicides but they can easily be tricked into swallowing poisoned bait."

"Any idea who laid the bait?"

"If I had, I'd be with Lieutenant Davies instead of you. Ratting, I believe it's called."

"On one of your colleagues at the museum?"

"I think a guard would be a viable hypothesis. The murderer must have known, to begin with, that Brown kept a fifth in his locker. He'd have to be able to gain access to the locker room without making himself conspicuous. That in itself mightn't be difficult since our only bathroom is next to the locker room and he could always pretend to be visiting the facilities. However" — Cousin Brooks paused impressively — "he'd also have to know which bottle belonged to Brown."

"Good point. He'd also have to know when it was safe to sneak back and switch the whiskey for the paint remover, and plant the note in Brown's pocket. Any idea where the paint remover came from, by the way?"

"Yes, it was mine. I repair some of the frames, as Dolores may have mentioned, and do other small jobs of that sort. I prefer the liquid paint remover to the viscous kind because the work is often delicate and I find it easier to control. The bottle was simply taken off my workbench, which is also in the basement, of course."

"Is that supposed to mean somebody's trying to frame the framer?"

"Oh, I hardly think so. That would be a bit too obvious, wouldn't it? I should be happy to know, though, that somebody isn't trying to kill me. That's why I felt I'd be well advised to have this little chat with you, sir. The police are showing an inclination to write Brown's death off as suicide. I don't want to be written off along with Brown."

"Have you any special reason to think you might be?"

"Only that ignorance is always dangerous.

Since I don't know why Witherspoon and Brown were killed, I have no idea whether or not my having been in the palazzo on both occasions may constitute a threat to the murderer."

"Cousin Brooks," cried Sarah, "you must give up that job this instant."

"What for?"

"Because I'd feel perfectly awful if anything happened to you."

"Out of respect for your sensibilities, then, I shall try to keep from being bumped off. Or is it rubbed out? As to the job, I don't think it's quite the done thing to walk out at a time like this. I'm sure Bittersohn understands my feeling. Speaking of walking, do you think it would be in order for me to ask Mrs. Sorpende out for a little stroll some evening soon? I thought she might care to observe the nighthawks."

"All right, Brooks, be a hero if you must. As to the nighthawks, Mrs. Sorpende loves to walk and I'm sure she'd be enraptured."

"And as to the museum," said Bittersohn, "just hang in there till we see what develops. I'm sending somebody over to have a look tomorrow. Keep me posted, and don't leave anything eatable or drinkable in your locker."

CHAPTER 8

The next night Mr. Bittersohn brought a guest back to dinner. The guest was not dressed for the occasion. In fact he was hardly dressed at all. In addition to the filthy poplin raincoat he shed on arriving, he wore a nondescript sports shirt, shrunken chino pants, and a pair of run-down loafers. Tie, socks, and undershirt were blatantly absent. His face, on the other hand, was modestly veiled in a three days' growth of blue-black whiskers. He was short, thin, and swarthy. His manners were polished as a duke's, and he talked volubly throughout the meal in a confidential murmur, leaning far over the table and waving a fork or a bit of bread in an exquisite little hand. Sarah's boarders, especially Jennifer LaValliere, found him entrancing.

So this was Bill Jones, the hot painting expert. Sarah wondered how soon Bill would approach her with a nice bargain in Vuillards.

After the ritual half hour for coffee in the library she went up to her sitting room, rather expecting that Bittersohn and his secret agent would soon follow. They did not. She'd just about decided that they'd gone downstairs to Bittersohn's room or that Jones had eloped with Miss LaValliere when they appeared, Bittersohn beckoning mysteriously as he eased the door open, Jones sliding along the walls and slipping noiselessly into the room. Sarah waited breathless for one of them to produce the Maltese Falcon.

Bill Jones, however, merely selected the seat farthest from the light, melted into the upholstery, and murmured almost inaudibly, "You called it, pal."

Bittersohn nodded. "What's your count?"

"I make it fifty-seven. Most professional job I ever saw."

"I don't suppose you'd care to tell me who's involved."

Bill shook his head. "Nobody I know."

"Bill, old buddy, this is Max you're talking to, remember?"

"Pal, I'm leveling. I don't know."

"But, Jesus, Bill, don't you even have a clue?"

Jones shook his curly black locks. "I even" — he waggled his dainty hands and looked from under his lids as if he were about to utter an impropriety — "like, you know, asked around. All I can tell you is it's a beautiful job. Clams by the bucket, man!"

Sarah could bear it no longer. "Would you two please tell me precisely what you're talking about?"

Both men looked at her as if she were somewhat feebleminded. "Bill was explaining," said Bittersohn, "that he has personal knowledge of fifty-seven originals from the Madam's that have been sold out of Boston, that he hasn't the faintest idea who stole them, and that the proceeds from the sales must have run into many millions of dollars unless the thief is an idiot, which doesn't seem possible. Where did the paintings go, Bill?"

"Around. You know."

"Any to New York?"

"No, too close. The guy's an artist," said Jones with due respect.

"Speaking of artists, who does the copies?"

Bill shrugged. "I don't know, but it's all one guy."

"You sure of that?"

Bill shrugged again.

"Sorry," Bittersohn apologized. "I didn't mean to offend you."

"But how could one person do so many?" cried Sarah. "I met someone who does that sort of thing and she says it takes ages because one has to be so careful about the details."

"Practically a life work," Bill agreed, "but it's been going on for a long time. That little Giotto hanging to the right of the fireplace in the music room was fenced on October first, 1959, through a sporting goods dealer named Mickey Brannigan down in the old neighborhood."

"Sporting goods dealer means a person who buys and sells stolen goods, Mrs. Kelling," Bittersohn explained before she could embarrass him by asking. "Mickey's dead now, I suppose."

"Su-ure. Long ago."

Otherwise Bill wouldn't have ratted, Sarah thought. She wondered what Brannigan had died of but thought she'd better not ask.

"How many of the Madam's paintings did Brannigan fence?" said Bittersohn.

"Just the one. Mickey wasn't an art man. He handled like general merchandise. I can't find anybody who's handled more than one or two."

"Then who makes the contacts? That's a hell of a job, Bill."

"You're telling me, Maxie? I wish I knew. I'd like to shake his hand. Or hers."

"You sure it's not theirs?"

"Look, pal, this little caper's been going on for a lot of years and there hasn't been a leak yet. Like they say, two people can keep a secret if one of them's dead, right?"

Bittersohn nodded. "Fifty-seven fakes, eh?"

"I'd say a lot more than fifty-seven, but that's your department. The Madam probably got stuck with a bunch of old ones in the first place. Fifty-seven originals fenced within the past thirty years and fifty-seven copies all from the same hand hanging in the palazzo now. That's all I can tell you for sure, Max. Well, I've got to blow. Thanks for dinner, Mrs. Kelling. Nice to have met you." He managed to convey a subtle impression that the meeting had been a great deal more than nice. "If I find out any more, Maxie, I'll be in touch."

"Do that. See you, Bill."

"Su-ure." Their guest slunk off down the back stairs, keeping in the shadows.

"I suppose he's on his way to some den of vice," Sarah observed rather wistfully.

Bittersohn shook his head. "As a matter of fact, he's going to a poetry reading at Wheelock College. How would you like to invite C. Edwald Palmerston to tea and crumpets or something?"

"You can't be serious! You have no idea what he's like."

"That's why I think it might be nice to get acquainted."

"Nice is not the operative word. If you'd said helpful or productive — "

"Okay, helpful or productive, so how about it?"

"If I must, but I'm not having him here without someone to back me up. Would Wednesday be good for you? That's Mrs. Sorpende's afternoon off."

Bittersohn raised an eyebrow. "Mrs. Sorpende's getting awfully indispensable around here all of a sudden. You wouldn't have been cutting her rent by any chance?"

"How clever of you! But she's such a darling and she's led such a rotten life and she makes so little at that tea shop and she does love it here. And if I let her go, Professor Ormsby would probably leave, too."

"Ormsby will be leaving in any case. He's a visiting professor, his year at MIT will be up in May, and he's got a wife and five kids in Michigan."

"Good heavens! Should I drop a hint to Mrs. Sorpende, do you think."

"If she doesn't already know, she'd better get out of the tea leaf business. Don't worry, Mrs. Sorpende's been taking care of herself a lot longer than you have. He hasn't been having an affair with her or anything, has he?"

"Not around here he hasn't. As far as I know he just sits and stares."

"Can't hang a man for that, can you? So you'll fix it up with Palmerston for Wednesday afternoon, right?"

"Will you promise faithfully to be here if he comes?"

"That's the object of the exercise. Not to put too fine a point on it, I want to shock him into hiring me to find out who's been pinching all the Madam's paintings. Then I'll also have a good excuse to keep an eye on your cousin Brooks."

"Oh, then of course I'll call him this minute."

Sarah had at last consented to Bittersohn's repeated urgings that she have an extension phone in her own room. She called from there and received such a fulsome response that she began to wonder if Lydia Ouspenska had, after all, known whereof she spoke regarding Palmerston and women. Bittersohn then went off on one of his mysterious bits of business and Sarah went downstairs to see if Mrs. Sorpende was still in the library and amenable to helping her entertain Brooks's new boss.

"I shall be delighted to do anything I can to further Mr. Brooks Kelling's career," the lady replied graciously. "He is a most knowledgeable man and a delightful conversationalist. His observations on the water ouzel and the ruby-crowned kinglet were highly educational, didn't you think? Perhaps you might allow me to make the sandwiches for tea? I do have professional experience in that line, you know, and I did so enjoy my little adventure in the kitchen on Sunday."

"We all enjoyed the results, and you certainly may. You'd better make plenty, though. Mr. Palmerston eats like a pig. And," Sarah added reflectively, "perhaps it might be a good idea to add a little ground glass to the fillings."

CHAPTER 9

Under different circumstances Sarah would have gone to considerable lengths to avoid having tea with C. Edwald Palmerston. Even as it was, she felt the need of some fresh air to brace herself for the ordeal. Around four o'clock, while Mrs. Sorpende was puttering happily around the kitchen and Mariposa was downstairs donning her jazzy orange uniform with new yellow and orange checked ribbons on the cap, Sarah put on her coat and strolled down to Charles Street.

Charles Street, the thoroughfare that runs through the bottom of Beacon Hill on the river side before you get to Storrow Drive and the Esplanade, is noted for its shops: florists' shops, food shops, boutiques of many sorts, and especially for its antique shops. One of these had a collection of china pug dogs in its window, all of whom appeared to be snarling. Sarah paused to snarl back. As she did, a movement inside the shop caught her eye.

What she'd seen were the exquisite little hands of Bill Jones, flying as they'd done at her own dinner table. She peeked in furtively, as she felt Bill would expect her to. His head was close to the antique dealer's ear. His lips were barely moving. Sarah had seen plenty of sign language while Aunt Caroline was still alive, though, and those eloquent gestures weren't hard for her to interpret. Bill was talking about paintings. Stolen paintings. Specifically, those paintings that had been taken from Madam Wilkins's palazzo.

A third man was in the cluttered room, lounging in a Savonarola armchair. Sarah recognized him, too. That was Bernie, the pianist who had done so much on Sunday to save Nick Fieringer's concert from total disaster. As far as she could see, he was reasonably sober.

Now what, if anything, did all this mean? Sarah knew the antique dealer slightly. In the grim days after Alexander's death, when she'd discovered she was flat broke and about to be foreclosed on for non-payment of mortgages she didn't know she'd inherited, she had gone to this Mr. Hayre in desperation with some of the family antiques. Would he have bought a stolen painting? Recalling what Mr. Hayre had paid her for a Canton tea set and what he'd subsequently sold it for, Sarah thought he probably would. She hurried back to the house, hoping to catch a private word with Mr. Bittersohn, but she got there too late. He was already in the library with Mrs. Sorpende and Mariposa was hovering in the wings, ready to do her stuff with the tea tray.

Punctually on the stroke of five, Mariposa showed C. Edwald Palmerston into the house. At two minutes past, he was bowing over the fair hand of Mrs. Sorpende. At three minutes past, Palmerston was still holding the aforesaid hand. At four minutes past Max Bittersohn coughed menacingly and Mr. Palmerston released his clutch.

"So good of you to invite me, Mrs. Kelling. Ah me, the last time I entered this house was to pay my respects at the time of your tragic loss. You appear to have made a speedy recovery," he added, looking askance at the flowered print dress Sarah had picked up for next to nothing in Filene's Basement under Mariposa's expert guidance because she was sick and tired of wearing her mother's old clothes.

"I'm trying to cope," Sarah replied. "Cream or lemon?"

"Milk please, and two lumps of sugar." Palmerston settled himself as close as he could get to Mrs. Sorpende and inhaled his refreshment with gusto.

"How are things going at the Madam's?" asked Bittersohn.

"The Madam's? I deplore that unfortunate nickname, Mr. Bittersohn. The Wilkins Museum merits the respect of our citizenry as one of Boston's most venerable institutions. I use the word venerable, of course, in the sense of meriting veneration. As to its actual age, I must confess that I myself can recall the opening, though dimly through the eyes of a mere babe. Ah, dear lady" — Palmerston seized this excuse to pat his neighbor's plump wrist — *"tempus fugit."*

"How right you are," said Mrs. Sorpende, edging herself ever so deftly out of reach and perhaps not being quite sure what *tempus fugit* meant but knowing it was generally safe to tell a man he was right.

"Would you happen to remember what the contents of the palazzo were appraised for at the time of the opening?" said Bittersohn.

"Madam Wilkins, to employ the title by which she chose to be known, was said to have spent well over ten million dollars on her paintings and other objets d'art. The value would be immeasurably higher now, needless to say."

"Would you care to bet on that?"

"I beg your pardon?"

"According to a recent independent survey," – Bittersohn had just retrieved a Matisse for the head of a local advertising agency – "there isn't twenty thousand dollars' worth of genuine stuff in the whole palazzo."

C. Edwald nearly bit a chunk out of a Spode teacup. "But – but that's preposterous! By what right do you – ?"

"You might say I've had the matter investigated because I'm a concerned citizen interested in preserving Boston's cultural treasures. I thought you, as chairman of the board of trustees, ought to be aware of the actual situation."

"Sir, if this is a joke I find it in poor taste. Who made this alleged survey?"

"Mrs. Kelling can testify that it's no joke, Mr. Palmerston. I happen to have taken my doctorate in art history. As a result of some things I noticed on a visit to the museum with Mrs. Kelling this past Sunday, I got an acquaintance who specializes in stolen paintings to go have a look. He drew up this list."

Bittersohn drew out a somewhat grubby sheet of expensive writing paper covered with calligraphy that would have passed muster in any medieval monastery. "As you can see, it shows which of your paintings have been replaced by copies within the past thirty years, and when and where each of the stolen originals passed out of the state. Quite an impressive piece of research, wouldn't you say?"

"I don't believe a word," said Palmerston, who had turned the color of a spoiled cauliflower.

"This morning," Bittersohn went on, "I gave a Xerox of this list to one of the curators of paintings at the Metropolitan Museum in New York, who happened to be in Boston on some other business. He spent several hours at the Wilkins and is willing to testify that at least twenty-five of the paintings listed here are modern copies. He didn't have time to go through the whole list, but he said he'd be willing to come back and have another crack at it."

"But — but, good heavens! Good heavens!"

"You'd better have another cup of tea, Mr. Palmerston."

"Tea? Good heavens, I – "

"Brandy, perhaps?" Mrs. Sorpende suggested.

"Yes, yes. Brandy by all means. Ordinarily I abstain but – yes, brandy. Please."

The man's color was ghastly. He leaned back against the sofa cushions as though his spine had given way, and sipped the drink Sarah brought him. After a minute or two, he made an effort to pull himself together.

"A curator from the Metropolitan, you say?"

"That's right," said Bittersohn. He mentioned a name. "Do you happen to know him?"

"Not personally, but the position would seem to place him as – ah – eminently reliable. I shall have to call a trustees' meeting forthwith. Or dare I? In so delicate a situation, perhaps the less said the better. The public must be protected from this dreadful allegation. We must lose not a moment. We must each pledge ourselves to secrecy here and now, and we must refrain above all from calling in the police and thus alerting the malefactors. A private detective, that's what we want! Someone of unexceptionable tact and discretion. Who was that chap my old friend Mrs. Forbot was telling

114

me about, who performed so capably in the case of the bogus Bellini at the Cotman Club? Let me think."

He snapped his long, bony fingers frantically. "It was some odd, foreign-sounding name."

"Bittersohn?" Sarah prompted.

"That's it. Why, it must have been you, Dr. Bittersohn. Well-met at Philippi, eh? Bravo! No wonder you interested yourself in the matter, and how right you were to call it to my attention in this private and discreet manner. I herewith place the situation in your hands. You will proceed with dispatch and, need I say, secrecy."

Old Anora Protheroe had once remarked, "Our lot aren't much for looks, by and large, but we're tough." With the resilience of one who has been brought up on Emerson, oatmeal porridge, codfish cakes, and Boston baked beans, C. Edwald Palmerston bounded to his feet, shook hands all around with a special lingering pressure for Mrs. Sorpende, thanked Sarah for her hospitality, urged Bittersohn to spare no effort, and left.

Mariposa took the teacups out to the kitchen. Mrs. Sorpende went up to change from her elegant tea gown into an even more elegant dinner gown. Sarah opened the library windows to air out C. Edwald Palmerston.

"Well, Mr. Bittersohn, I hope you got what you wanted."

He came over to help her with the windows. "I did. Tell you what, since you've been such a good kid I'll take you out to see the nighthawks after dinner."

"I've seen nighthawks, thank you."

"Then come for the exercise. It will do you good."

"Perhaps you're right."

In any event, Sarah went. Mr. Bittersohn's idea of a quiet evening stroll was not what she'd been used to. He led her through the byways behind Park Square to a place she'd never been before. Dolph would have called it a dive and for all Sarah knew about such things he might well have been right. They were sitting in a booth listening to three elderly ladies perform with verve on the saxophone, the drums, and the double bass when they were joined by an acquaintance.

"Ah, my God, the beautiful Max and his adorable sweetheart!"

"Hi, Lydia," said the beautiful Max. "Can we buy you a drink?"

"But of course." Countess Ouspenska squeezed herself in beside Sarah. "I will sit with this little one so you can look at us both. In such a rotten light as here I am still passable. Double vodka please, Giovanni, from the bottle you didn't water yet."

Lydia got her drink, took a mighty swig, and gasped. "Peachy! Today I finish my genuine antique masterpiece and get a beautiful present from an old goat and now the magnificent Max buys me a double vodka. Is life in the old bat yet, not?"

"I think you're wonderful," Sarah replied with all sincerity.

"Little darling, I love you madly!" Countess Ouspenska embraced her seatmate with Slavic fervor, transferring a good deal of pancake makeup to Sarah's flawless cheek. "Listen, do you know what that old goat Palmerston does? He sends a basket of goodies so big" – she flung out her arms in a wild jangle of bracelets – "with a note in fond remembrance. Is the first time that old foxy-loxy ever puts anything in writing. Too bad he doesn't sign it." She took another gulp of her drink. "Anyway, this week I eat."

"How nice for you."

"You said it, babushka. Now I negotiate for sale of my wonderful icon and for one month I have it made in the shade. Is like song be like I hold your head up high somewhere is a bluejay of happiness."

"What's this about your icon, Lydia?" Bittersohn asked ever so casually.

The countess giggled. "Is my secret. Maybe you come to my studio without this pretty little watchdog and ask me again nice, eh?"

"Sounds like a great idea to me. How about another?"

"Unfortunately no. I have to stay bright-eyed and bushy-tailed. Is important business appointment." The countess stifled a hiccup with an aristocratic gesture and sorted out her scarves and necklaces. "I go now."

"Can we drop you somewhere?"

"No, is better for security I go alone. Please case the joint to see is anybody follow."

Bittersohn pulled his coat collar up around his face and tiptoed to the door. "Sst, Lydia!" His whisper carried easily over the saxophone, the drums, and the double bass. "The coast is clear."

"Good. In my new business is necessary to take precautions. Was necessary in my old business, too. *Au revoir,* my little wood pigeon. You come and see me too. I paint you as madonna and child in authentic Byzantine technique."

Countess Ouspenska pulled one of her scarves far down over her face, put on a pair of dark glasses, and slithered out. Bittersohn came back to the booth and helped Sarah into her coat.

"Come on, we'll follow her by stealth and cunning. She'd be heartbroken if we didn't. Try to look furtive."

They had no trouble keeping the countess in sight. She must have made a few more stops before she met them, for she was making almost as much leeway as headway although her general bearing was more or less in the direction of Charles and Beacon.

"I'll bet she's heading for that antique shop," Sarah murmured.

"What antique shop?"

"The one where I saw your friend Bill Jones this afternoon."

"Huh? Which shop was this?"

"The one with all the china dogs in the window. It's run by a Mr. Hayre, who gypped me so unmercifully on the Canton tea set."

"What was Bill doing?"

"Whispering into Mr. Hayre's ear about the paintings at the Madam's."

"How do you know?"

"I could tell by the way he was waving

his hands around. That piano player of Mr. Fieringer's was there, too."

"Bernie? What the hell? Did they see you?"

"I think not. I was outside peeking through the window."

"Why?"

"Masochism, I suppose. I always look in when I pass the store, to see if he has any of my things on sale for about sixty times what he paid me for them. Look, she is heading for Charles Street."

Countess Ouspenska must have been revived by the exercise. She had got up steam and was progressing at a much faster rate. She managed to nip across Beacon just as the light changed, while the two who were following her had to wait till the traffic stopped. By the time they could go again, she was nowhere in sight.

"Damn, we've lost her," muttered Bittersohn.

"No we haven't." Sarah took his hand and hustled him up a tiny alley and around a corner.

"Where are we?" he whispered.

"Behind Mr. Hayre's antique shop, of course."

"And what do we do now?"

"Lurk."

CHAPTER 10

Sarah's hunch was a good one. They'd been peering down the alley from behind the ashcans for barely ten minutes when they saw the countess emerge. She had a man with her. As the couple passed beneath one of the imitation gas lamps that help to give Charles Street its Old Boston atmosphere, the lurkers in the shadows could see he was Bernie the piano player. Perhaps Lydia had got paid for her icon. Anyway, either she or Bernie must be in funds for they hailed a taxi.

"Come on." Bittersohn practically carried Sarah across to a rank where, luckily, another cab was idling. "Mind following that cabbie who just pulled out?" he said to the driver. "We were supposed to meet that couple who are riding with him but they must have got tired of waiting just as we came along. We're all going to the same party and they forgot to give us the address."

"Well, that's life," said the cabbie in a fine burst of philosophical originality. "I could pull up alongside and ask."

"No, we'll follow along and surprise them. It shouldn't be too far. Somewhere around Brookline Village, I think. Anyway, we wouldn't mind having a little time to ourselves, if you get what I mean."

The driver must have got what he meant, for he turned up the volume on his radio and shut the opening in the heavy plastic that separated the front seat from the back. Bittersohn grinned and pulled Sarah close to him.

"Mind if we act natural?" he murmured.

"Is this what you naturally do with women in taxis?" she whispered back, not making any real attempt to pull away.

"We're a guy and his date on our way to a party, remember?"

"Do you suppose we really are? On our way to a party, I mean? Where is Bernie taking the countess, do you suppose?" Sarah found it necessary to remind herself of the object of their mission. Being this close to Mr. Bittersohn might otherwise divert a young widow's attention to matters she had no business thinking about.

"I guessed Brookline Village because that

seems to be where it's at these days, and that's more or less where we're heading, but don't ask me why. Right now the only thing I like about this expedition is having you along, and I'm not sure I was smart to bring you. There are only two things Bernie can do by himself: play the piano and drink. Otherwise he waits for Nick Fieringer to lay it out for him. His hanging around that antique shop, which seems to be another place where it's at, could mean that he's running errands for Nick."

"And what would that mean?"

"Mrs. Kelling, you were there when Nick tried to tout me off this Wilkins business on Sunday evening. I don't know whether coming to me was his own idea or if somebody sent him. I expect he'd take a buck to do an errand. Nick has a million pals, but as far as making a living goes, he must be just about scraping by."

"You don't think he'd murder two guards as a favor to a friend?"

"Not Nick. He's too fat and clumsy, for one thing."

"Could he have told Bernie to do it?"

"How could Bernie have been up on the third floor pushing Joe Witherspoon over the balcony when he had to go directly to the

Tintoretto Room as soon as he finished playing and have his hand held by somebody's great-aunt the music lover?" Bittersohn absentmindedly closed his own hand more snugly around Sarah's. "Furthermore, I can't see Nick trusting Bernie to load Brown's bottle. Bernie would have been too apt to drink up the murder weapon himself."

"Mr. Fieringer would have been able to manage that business with the bottle easily enough, wouldn't he? As for Witherspoon, well, he did like painted ladies."

"Not Lydia Ouspenska's kind, if that's what you're getting at. Anyway, your Cousin Brooks would surely have seen and remembered her. Lydia's not just another face in the crowd, you know."

"But what if she was already upstairs when Brooks came on duty and he never saw her? Mr. Fieringer could have let her in, couldn't he? He probably has access to the museum during off-hours because of having to arrange things about the concerts, don't you think? Then she could have dashed through the chapel and got out somehow while we were down among all that confusion in the courtyard. Brown could have seen her and done his robbery act to make it look as if he didn't suspect her, and been killed because he actually did. Oh dear, I wish I hadn't thought of that."

Being in a strategic position to offer comfort, Bittersohn did. "Wait a minute, you can't start playing favorites. I like old Lydia, too, but what you just said makes a certain amount of sense. You told me she did a perfect job on that icon. Being an artist yourself, you'd be a pretty fair judge. If she's that good a copyist we can't eliminate her as the person who faked the paintings. Bill says it's all the work of one person and Lydia's been around a long time. She may have branched out into icons because there's nothing left over there worth copying."

Sarah rubbed her cheek on the handsome gray worsted topcoat she was being clasped against. She'd never before been embraced by an attractive man in a taxicab. Alexander had always taken her on the subway and would have shied away from a public demonstration of affection in any case. It was too bad she couldn't relax and enjoy the experience, but of course that wasn't what she was here for.

"I suppose the countess might have been able to wangle a key to the museum out of Mr. Palmerston while they were having that love affair or whatever it was."

"Would you run through that again slowly, please?"

"I told you she'd been on close terms with him at one time. Didn't you understand what she was saying tonight about old foxy-loxy sending her caviar and whatnot in fond remembrance? She told me practically in so many words that day I went to her studio that they used to — you know."

"How would I know?" said Bittersohn virtuously. "You mean people do those things with people they're not married to?"

"Not in taxis." Sarah straightened up and pulled her skirt down over her knees. Not knowing the customary procedure in this sort of situation she couldn't be sure, but it did seem to her that things were getting a bit out of hand.

Bittersohn took the hint and loosened his grip, though only by a little. "I should send my ears out to be laundered. If that's the case, Lydia could easily have dropped a question here and there about which pictures were worth stealing, what times the guards were off duty, and other useful bits of information while his mind was, as one might say, otherwise occupied. And she could have pinched his keys while he had his pants off and made impressions on a cake of soap.

She'd get a bang out of that."

"I daresay she would," Sarah had to agree.

"So now Palmerston's chasing her again?"

"Well, no. Actually I was the one who sent the caviar."

"What in hell for?"

"Because she had no money and not a bite to eat in the house except a few sandwiches left over from Mrs. Tawne's tea party. Besides, I thought it might be interesting to see what happened."

"Woman, you're not safe to have around."

However, Bittersohn showed no inclination to let her go until the taxi lurched through a last horrendous pothole, crossed the line into Brookline, where the roads immediately became faultless, and clanked to a stop.

As he had predicted, they'd wound up in Brookline Village. A bearded man who must have been a hippie, a yippie, or perhaps a flower child back in the sixties and was still trying to keep the torch alight stood in front of a dilapidated block of storefront flats yelling, "Lee-roy! Hey, Lee-roy!"

From above came sounds of guitars and bongos and sonorous blats that suggested somebody was either keeping beef cattle in his apartment or practicing scales on a sousaphone. Somebody else was playing

Handel's Second Concerto Grosso on a stereo that was considerably more hi than fi. Somebody was singing, somebody was fighting, somebody was chanting in Tibetan. Nobody appeared to be just sitting around and letting it all hang out.

Bittersohn paid off their cab while the pair they'd followed were doing the same. Then he yelled, "Hey, Bernie!"

"Yay, Maxie," the pianist bellowed back. "Where you for, man?"

"I was looking for Leroy but he doesn't seem to be around."

The bearded one on the sidewalk stopped shouting. "Hey man, you see Leroy you tell him I'm like in Joy's pad." He shuffled off.

"I wonder who Leroy is?" Sarah murmured.

"A friend of that fay cat's," said Bittersohn. "Who's the beard, Bernie?"

"Some friend of Leroy's, I guess. Maxie, you know Lydia. Lydia, this is Maxie's old lady, the society broad."

"I am acquaint with Maxie's old lady," said Countess Ouspenska gaily. "We amuse ourselves together among the proletariat, no? Come, little one, I show the way. Please to *en garde* for broken steps."

As they groped their way up the unlighted stairway into a loft that had been more or less partitioned off with painters' tarpaulins hung on wires, the beat of bongo drums was stilled. Fifteen pairs of oversized sunglasses were turned on the unparalleled apparition of a man with a shave and a haircut, a London tailored suit, a clean shirt, and a silk foulard necktie of restrained pattern. The fact that he was also wearing shoes disturbed them almost to a frenzy. At last, however, somebody shrugged and muttered, "Like everybody got to do his own thing, right?" and the bongos started again.

Bernie and Lydia flopped on what appeared to be the remains of a sofa and shoved someone else off to make room for Sarah. As she was wearing a thirty-year-old coat of her mother's, she didn't appear to frighten them as Bittersohn had. She herself was a bit dismayed, however, when her escort disappeared behind one of the tarpaulins.

At first she didn't know what to do, so she just sat and tried not to inhale too deeply. Then she became aware that a current of excitement was swirling through the fetid atmosphere and she began to wonder if by any chance Bittersohn could be the generator. Her suspicion was confirmed when a character who happened to be sitting on her feet remarked to the character who'd been kicked off the sofa, "Man, we got a live one aboard."

"What you mean, man?"

"Like Santa Claus is coming to town, man. Like the rhomboid with the rubles, man. He digs art, man. Like paintings, like that."

"So who paints, man?"

"Who don't, man? Like Leroy and Bengo and Cynthia."

"Cynthia don't paint. He sculps."

"So who can tell? Man, I got to show this cat my collages."

"Man, you got no collages."

"Time I get that cat over to my pad, man, I got collages. Empty a wastebasket into a puddle of glue, man, you got a collage."

"Man, you got no wastebasket."

"Man, you got no higher vision. Me, I dig them genuine steel engravings like Abraham Jackson and Ulysses S. G-note. Fare thee well, man. I go to cut me a piece of the action."

He or she scrambled to his or her feet and went in quest of the rhomboid with the rubles. Above the pandemonium Sarah could now pick out Bittersohn's usually agreeable baritone, now sounding pompous, moderately drunk, and a touch imbecilic. "Of course I also collect recognized masters," he was saying as he crawled back under the tarpaulin, trailed by at least half a dozen unrecognized geniuses.

"Man, how you like to collect a genuine Mondrian?" urged a short, wiry type with a ferocious Fu Manchu mustache and chin whisker.

"Man, that Lupe is a gas," muttered the cynic who was now sprawled across Sarah's left foot. "He copies them Mondrians off the linoleum at Sears and Sawbuck. Man, I say a real creative artist ought to think up his own Mondrians."

"Lupe ain't an artist, he's an operator," said the body now sprawled across Sarah's right foot. "Man, he can smell a live one all the way to Charlestown. Like he goes to one of them cut-rate supermarkets, dig, and buys a case of oregano and bums the use of somebody's oven and like dries it out till it gets good and brown. Then he peddles it for grass."

"Man, that ain't right." The left-foot sprawler took what was left of a very homemade-looking cigarette from his or her lips and regarded the roach sadly. "Man, like I was really beginning to elevate."

Nobody was paying any attention whatever to Sarah. Lydia had betaken herself elsewhere. Bernie was dozing with a drink in his hand, the glass tilted dangerously toward Sarah's lap. She reached over to take it out of harm's reach and he opened one scarlet-rimmed eye. "Who're you?"

"I'm Maxie's old lady, the society broad," she replied. "Don't you remember? You introduced me to Lydia downstairs."

"Oh, yeah. I'm not talkin'."

"I can see you're not."

"What are you, some kind of a wise society broad? I'm not sayin' a word, see? Not one word," he bellowed.

"I'm not asking you to," Sarah replied, somewhat alarmed.

"He tol' me. He said don't tell Max."

"But I'm not Max."

"Whadda you mean, you're not Max?" Bernie rubbed his eyes and took a closer look. "Hey, you're not Max. You're Maxie's old lady. I gotta look out for Max."

"Who says so?"

"Who says what?"

"Look out for Max."

"Thass ri'. Look out for Max." Bernie dropped the glass and went back to sleep.

Sarah moved as far as she could get from the wet spot made by the spilled drink and puzzled over this interesting vignette. If

Bernie wasn't supposed to tell Max, then Bernie must know something Bittersohn would want to hear. But who would be fool enough to entrust a secret to a lush like Bernie? Lydia Ouspenska might, but whatever else she was or could have been, the countess was definitely not a he. As for the rest of this lot, they might be males, females, or androgynous for all Sarah could tell. However, none of them appeared to have any previous acquaintance with Bittersohn or any reason to have expected he'd show up here, so why would they have warned the pianist against him?

Sarah had a sudden vivid picture of those flying, delicate hands in the antique shop. Bernie had sat there watching while Bill Jones whispered into Mr. Hayre's ear. Musicians were used to interpreting gestures made by conductors; maybe Bernie had read Bill's gestures as Sarah herself had. Maybe Bernie had let Bill know that he'd learned what was supposed to have been kept from his ears and maybe it was Bill who'd told him not to tell Max. Tell Max what? Jones had been most obliging about coming up with the information Bittersohn wanted about the stolen paintings. Maybe he'd been equally considerate in letting the other side know that Bittersohn was on the trail.

Perhaps she was just bored with being ignored for so long, but it seemed terribly important to let Bittersohn know at once what Bernie had said. Sarah tried to wriggle over to him but he was now surrounded by a solid phalanx of artists and their self-appointed agents, every one bent on cutting himself a slice of the action. Several were insisting that this new fairy godfather go somewhere to look at something.

"But I don't want to break up the party," he was protesting.

"You won't, man. We'll like take it with us."

Somebody grabbed the bongo drums, somebody else grabbed the wine jug. The throng surged out into the street, leaving Bernie sleeping alone on the sofa.

During the confusion Sarah managed somehow to reach Bittersohn. He grabbed her by the waist and held on. "Stay close to me," he muttered. "God knows what we've got ourselves into."

"I have to talk to you," she panted. "I have to tell you something."

"Save it."

He guided her as best he could up a staircase even more depressing than the first.

They found themselves in what at least looked like an artist's studio, of sorts. In one corner stood a neat stack of authentic Sears Roebuck Mondrians. Lupe spread his wares and made his spiel. Bittersohn admired but did not buy. A more or less female-looking person who might have been Mrs. Lupe but probably wasn't displayed a number of shirt cardboards with bits of old toothpaste tubes adhering to them. Bittersohn asked mildly if anyone happened to be working in a more traditionally representational manner.

"How about a Rembrandt?" offered the versatile Lupe.

"Ah, the very thing I was looking for. Where is it?"

"Hey, Bengo, what did you do with that painting of the fat old broad in the rocking chair?"

"Me I done nothin', man. You unloaded it to that cowboy from Milwaukee who wanted a real, live Toulouse-Lautrec."

"Oh, yeah, I forgot. Look, man" – Lupe turned back to his prey – "you come back in three days I have a jazzy Rembrandt for you. Any special subject you got in mind?"

"Well – er – what would you suggest?"

"How about a nice fat old broad in a rocking chair?"

"I thought Toulouse-Lautrec painted the broads in rocking chairs."

"Sure, he got the idea from Rembrandt. Only Rembrandt, see, he puts in a cat."

"Hey, a broad and a cat takes more than three days, man," Bengo protested.

"I don't mean a cat, man, I mean a pussycat. Like with the fur and the whiskers and the whole bit. Like Leroy's pussycat."

"I don't want Leroy's pussycat in my Rembrandt," Bittersohn objected pettishly. "I want Rembrandt's pussycat."

"Man, you got to be reasonable, dig?" said Bengo. "Where we goin' to get Rembrandt's pussycat?"

"Where are you going to get Rembrandt's old lady?"

"Look, man," Lupe interjected, "like leave the technical details to us. You want Rembrandt's pussycat you get Rembrandt's pussycat, dig?"

"But how am I to know it's an authentic Rembrandt pussycat?" Bittersohn pouted.

Lupe turned on his customer a look of outraged virtue. "Man, you can trust *me!*"

"Just don't buy any of his marijuana," Sarah could not refrain from murmuring. "Er — dear — " she couldn't very well address him as Mr. Bittersohn and she felt diffident about saying Max — "don't you think we've trespassed on these nice people's hospitality long enough for one evening?"

"Yes, my love. I must give Mr. Lupe and Mr. Bengo a small deposit on the Rembrandt. If this lady has quite finished with my wallet — " Bittersohn deftly tweaked his sharkskin billfold from the folds of a nearby poncho and extracted two five-dollar bills. "Thank you, ladies and gentlemen, for a pleasant and instructive evening. Come, dearest."

"Wait, I go with you," cried Countess Ouspenska.

"But," hissed Sarah, "I — "

"Yes, darling, as soon as we get home. We'd be delighted to have your company, Countess."

"What about Bernie?" Sarah asked him, now greatly annoyed. "Shall I go back and get him, too?"

"Is not necessary," said the countess. "Bernie will sleep as good in the pad of these cats as in his own. They are equally moldy. Come, little flower of the snow, we find a taxi. The magnificent Max will pay. He is so rich for Rembrandts he has also money for taxi. I do not dig you this evening, *mon ami*."

"I guess I'm just not myself. How come you're hanging out with that motley crew, Lydia?"

"Me, I am bohemian. Is no bohemia around Boston any more. The arsonists burn it all down. Also those frowsy middle-aged hippies look so awful is good for my ego. To be formerly beautiful woman on the skids is depressing. I confess this to you because I am drunk. Even to get drunk is not so easy these days. With this moldy pack of cats is at least free liquor though not good unless stolen."

"Who steals it?"

"Anybody, no doubt. Is not hard to shoplift in baggy clothing."

"What do they steal besides liquor?"

Lydia shrugged. "What not? Lupe says is less bourgeois to steal than to work. I have not the knack. Also is not becoming in titled aristocrat of high-class family to sneak always from the fuzz."

"This Lupe man seems to be quite an enterprising character," Sarah remarked.

"He has in the fire many irons, yes. Is expensive to be a bum."

"Are Bengo's Rembrandts any good?" Bittersohn wanted to know.

"Good enough for the tourists off the

sight-seeing buses."

"They don't come up to the ones at the Madam's, eh?"

"Why do you say Madam's? Is bad luck that place." Lydia made the sign of the horns and spat three times over her left shoulder. "I say no more."

Incredibly, she didn't. They found a cab on Washington Street and got her into it. By the time they pulled up in front of the Fenway Studios, she was nodding heavily on Sarah's collarbone.

"She feels like the White Queen." Sarah shook her burden. "Countess Ouspenska, wake up. You're home."

"Go away," moaned the sign painter's daughter from Chelsea. "I say no more."

"Damn," said Bittersohn. "She's out like a light. Here, help me get her arm around my shoulder and let's see how good she is at sleepwalking. Come on, Lydia, old sport."

It was as well Countess Ouspenska didn't eat more regularly. Thin as she was, they had a struggle to get her up to her studio. "Look in her handbag," panted Bittersohn. "Get her door key."

Sarah rummaged with distaste in the mad jumble. "There's so much junk — good God, look at this!"

Amid the welter of lipstick stubs, soiled tissues, and unpaid bills lay a neat little snub-nosed revolver. Bittersohn picked it up and broke open the chamber. The gun was fully loaded.

"Whatever shall we do?" Sarah wondered.

"Put it back where you found it. Has she a permit in her bag?"

"I can't go prowling through her personal papers."

"I can."

"Then wait till we get her parked somewhere. Oh, good, I think I've found a key."

"I've got news for you. The door was unlocked all the time." Bittersohn turned the knob and pushed it open. Getting the countess down that short flight of stairs and through the clutter of furniture below was no small chore. When they stumbled across a divan, Sarah panted, "Can't we leave her here?"

"Sure." Bittersohn eased the inert form down on the lumpy plush.

"Poor old thing." Sarah looked down at the gaunt figure so bravely decked out in tight black pants and a garish nylon jersey. "I'm going to take off some of this jewelry. She clanks every time she moves. See if you can find a blanket."

She slipped off a pound or two of chains and bangles, removed the run-over gold sandals, then covered Lydia with the worn velvet throw Bittersohn brought from the inner room.

"Okay, let's go," he whispered.

"But I thought you wanted to snoop."

"Not now." He took Sarah's hand and guided her back up the stairs. When they were out in the hall with the door shut, he explained, "Lydia has company. I found a man asleep in her bed."

"Who was it?"

"I don't know. It was too dark to see and I thought it might be rude to turn on the light."

"Perhaps it was Mr. Palmerston." Sarah giggled nervously. "I wonder if she knew he was there. One would think she'd have stayed at home if she was expecting company. That sort of company, at any rate."

"One might also think she'd be a little more careful about locking her door if she's packing that gun for protection. I wish some of this would make a grain of sense."

"Oh, but it does," said Sarah. "That's what I was trying to tell you back at that pad place when you kept shushing me up. It's Mr. Hayre, just as I thought."

"What makes you so sure?"

"Bernie told me somebody warned him not to talk to you."

"I see. That makes everything clear as crystal."

"Don't be so snippy. I told you I'd seen Bill Jones talking to Mr. Hayre in his shop this afternoon and that Bernie was there, too. Then tonight Lydia went to the shop and came out with Bernie, so he may have been there ever since I saw him, mayn't he? So when Bernie said tonight that he'd been warned not to tell you something I knew it had to be either Bill Jones or Mr. Hayre who warned him. So that must mean — I suppose it doesn't actually have to mean a great deal, does it?"

"Time will tell," said Bittersohn. "I hope that cab's still waiting."

It was. As they walked toward it they could hear voices from the parking lot behind the building.

"Wait in the cab, will you?" Bittersohn darted around the corner. In less than a minute he was back. "It's Palmerston and Jimmy Agnew, Dolores Tawne's brother. They were getting into what I assume is Palmerston's car."

"So late? Mrs. Tawne must have been

giving them a high old time. She's besotted about that man, though I can't imagine why."

"Everybody looks good to somebody. Tulip Street, please, driver."

"Speaking of good looks, I think I'm going to have to do something about my clothes," Sarah remarked, feeling a little uncomfortably that light conversation might be in order now that they weren't a guy and his date on their way to a party. "All those people took me for your mother."

"The hell they did!"

"Well, they kept calling me your old lady."

"That's not what they meant."

"Then what did they mean?"

Bittersohn cleared his throat. "Old lady is a sort of general description for a woman of any age with whom a man happens to be living."

"I see. I suppose the countess told them —" Sarah reflected on what the countess would have been most likely to tell them and decided she'd better let the subject drop. After that neither of them said much except, "Good night."

CHAPTER 11

Sarah woke early from force of habit but she still felt sleepy and confused. Had she or had she not been dreaming about finding a revolver in Countess Ouspenska's handbag and being mistaken for Mr. Bittersohn's old lady? And was this the night she'd invited Cousin Brooks to dinner? Recalled to domestic concerns, she bounded out of bed, took a quick shower, and did her baby-fine light brown hair up into a landladyish knot.

Now that she was fully awake, she had a vivid memory of how Mr. Bittersohn had kept rubbing his cheek against that same hair most of the way from Charles Street to Brookline Village and how she hadn't tried to make him stop. Of course he'd only been doing it as part of the act they were putting on, so why did the mere memory get her so hot and bothered, and whatever was she going to say to him at breakfast?

As it happened, she didn't get to say

much of anything. Bittersohn was never among the early birds and they'd have been well chaperoned in any case. By the time she'd sent Mr. Porter-Smith off to his job at third cousin Percy Kelling's accountancy firm, Miss LaValliere to her classes at Katy Gibbs, Professor Ormsby to his aerodynamics laboratory at MIT, and Mrs. Gates to a lecture on Chinese embroideries at the Art Museum, Mrs. Sorpende was down with a new hairdo and an air of happy expectancy.

"I believe it is this evening your cousin comes to dinner?" she remarked. "Do you think he will remember?"

"Oh, yes. Brooks is looking forward to it, I'm sure. He mentioned particularly that he'd like to discuss the nighthawks with you."

"Nighthawks?"

"Yes, you know those birds with the bent-back wings that fly around in the evening going, 'peent, peent.'"

"Dear me, is that what they are? I fear I have a great deal to learn about ornithology."

"I'm sure Brooks will be happy to teach you."

"He is so kind."

Mrs. Sorpende touched her napkin daintily to her lips and permitted her cup to be refilled from the graceful silver coffee urn. She was still dawdling at the table when Mr. Bittersohn appeared, helped himself to eggs and toast at the buffet, said "Thanks" when Sarah handed him a cup of coffee, ate quickly, and left. Mrs. Sorpende smiled her Gioconda smile, nodded with what Sarah could have sworn was an air of satisfaction, and said she must be wending her way.

Sarah couldn't understand what Mrs. Sorpende was looking so pleased about. She herself was in a bit of a state. What was ailing the man? Considering the way he'd behaved last night in the taxi, and all the dears and darlings he'd thrown around so freely out there in Brookline Village she'd have thought — well, she oughtn't to be thinking such things so soon after her bereavement anyway. And perhaps Mr. Bittersohn had come to the conclusion that she was a flighty woman who needed to be put in her place.

Or perhaps he had a toothache or a hangover, although she'd thought his air of inebriety was camouflage for the benefit of those strange people who were going to sell him the Rembrandt as soon as Bengo got it painted. Or perhaps he hadn't slept well. He looked as if he hadn't. Did he go out again last night after he brought her home? She wished she dared ask Mariposa, who had come to clear up and was wondering, no doubt, why Sarah was still sitting there alone over a cup of cold coffee when it was her turn to wash the dishes.

But she didn't. It would seem too much like prying. It would also seem as if she were showing too much interest in Mr. Bittersohn and she might as well face it, she was. Sarah got up and went to do the dishes.

"By the way," she remarked to Mariposa over the sink, "my Cousin Brooks will be here for dinner tonight."

"Is that the little guy who came Sunday with the old battle-ax?"

"That's right, you missed him, didn't you? I suppose Charles told you."

"Yeah." Mariposa handed over more coffee cups. "He said your cousin was a fine gentleman but the old bat he had with him was for the birds."

"Actually Brooks is the one for the birds. I mean he goes out bird-watching and does bird calls and that sort of thing."

"Oh, yeah? I got an uncle can imitate a cockfight."

"Perhaps you hadn't better mention that to Brooks. He takes a dim view of cockfights.

So do I, if it comes to that."

"Well, there's your old culture barrier for you. What we going to feed this bird cat?"

"I thought I'd make chicken paprika."

"How about that? If he's so hung up on birds, how come he eats chicken?"

"Perhaps he doesn't. I never thought. Anyway we'll have noodles and string beans amandine with it, and a carrot pudding. He can fill up on those." By mere coincidence, Mr. Bittersohn happened to be particularly fond of chicken paprika, noodles, string beans amandine, and carrot pudding.

Sarah had been so busy with other things the past few days that she'd got behind on domesticity. She buckled down to her chores, taking a little extra time to freshen the plants in Mr. Bittersohn's room and sew a button on his pajamas. This was not a service usually provided to the paying guests, but there was the button on the floor and there were the pajamas on the bed and it wasn't as though she'd never mended a man's pajamas before.

So why was she making such a production of it this time? She bit off the thread rather angrily, folded the garment and laid it at the foot of the bed, whacked up the fat red and blue print pillows that were supposed to make the room look more like a studio apartment than a mere bedroom, and went upstairs to grind carrots for the pudding.

At six o'clock Sarah was in the library wearing her gray satin dinner gown and Granny Kay's bluebird pin. A minute or so later Brooks arrived, neat as a penguin in the dinner jacket he'd got when he entered Harvard, Class of '46. He accepted a glass of the sherry Charles got somewhere at a cut rate with no questions asked and none answered, and told Miss LaValliere a good deal more about the lesser auk than she probably wanted to know. Then Mrs. Sorpende arrived in her new peach-colored lace gown with rust-colored satin ribbons and Miss LaValliere was ever so gently let off the hook.

By the time they sat down to dinner it was clear that Brooks by himself was an even greater success than when he'd been encumbered by Mrs. Tawne. Mrs. Gates, herself a life member of the Audubon Society, was glad to hear his views on the nesting habits of the least bittern. Mr. Porter-Smith found him a kindred spirit, ready for a waspish exchange of minutiae on any subject whatsoever. Mr. Bittersohn came in late and silent, but warmed up as he ate his chicken paprika. They had a fire in the library while they drank their coffee and all was merry until Charles came in and announced, "Mr. Palmerston is here, madam."

"Here where?" Sarah asked him crossly.

"In the front hall at the moment, madam."

"What on earth does he want? Did he ask for Mr. Bittersohn?"

"No, madam, he merely wished to be announced."

"Then you might as well show him in and bring another cup."

If he'd come for a progress report, Palmerston appeared in no hurry to get it. He barely acknowledged the presence of his two temporary employees, bowed slightly to Miss LaValliere and Mrs. Gates and not at all to Professor Ormsby or Mr. Porter-Smith, then settled himself on the sofa beside Mrs. Sorpende and engaged in what he must mean to be amiable pleasantries. Brooks Kelling, on the other side of the lady, edged closer and commenced a diversionary operation of considerable finesse.

The gracious lady behaved admirably as usual, parrying Mr. Palmerston's heavy-handed compliments with genteel banalities and sympathizing with Mr. Kelling over the sad plight of the whooping crane, while

Professor Ormsby sat and glared.

Mrs. Sorpende's charms were ample enough for two, but with three admirers practically crawling into her lap at once, she began to show the strain. Bittersohn roused himself from his private concerns and was gallanty trying to draw Palmerston's fire with a reference to the Wilkins Museum when Charles entered the room again, looking as if someone had slipped him a page from the wrong script. His voice actually cracked a bit as he announced, "Countess Ouspenska."

Bittersohn and Sarah exchanged startled glances. Palmerston reared back like a stricken wolverine. The rest, except for Professor Ormsby, who was still rapt in contemplation of those bits of Mrs. Sorpende that were visible through the interstices of the peach-colored lace, straightened up and looked expectant.

Mrs. Gates had traveled extensively in her younger days and met lots of countesses but not even she, no doubt, had ever encountered one like Lydia. Tonight the icon painter had on a long dress of eggplant-colored sailcloth painted with genuine Byzantine motifs. Makeup and dime-store jewelry were laid on with wild abandon. Still her regal bearing and haggard beauty, mercifully enhanced by the firelight, made an impact that brought most of the company to their feet.

Sarah of course went forward to greet her guest and present her boarders. Miss LaValliere, despite the skimpiness of her skirt, managed a creditable curtsey. Mrs. Sorpende, having so much more to work with, did even better. Mrs. Gates, being old enough, rich enough, and well-born enough not to bother, nevertheless honored Countess Ouspenska with a smile and an inclination of her lovely white head.

Mr. Porter-Smith bowed smartly from the hips and kissed the noble hand. So did Mr. Bittersohn, with an ever so slight wink in Sarah's direction. Even Professor Ormsby managed a nod and a grunt. Brooks Kelling earned a glance of admiration from Mrs. Sorpende by shaking hands and saying "Hello, Lydia, glad to see you."

"And of course you know Mr. Palmerston," Sarah finished mischievously.

"Ho ho, do I not? His remembrance is more fondly than mine but I forgive much for the sake of that caviar."

Needless to say, Palmerston was nonplussed. "I'm afraid I don't follow you," he stammered.

Lydia shrugged. "Neither does anybody else any more. Is hell to get old and ugly."

Miss LaValliere giggled. Sarah said quickly, "We're having coffee, Countess. May Charles bring you a cup? And will you have something to eat with it?"

"Thank you, coffee only. Tonight I have dine on caviar and blini. I take raincheck for when things are not so aye-aye-aye, eh?"

"Of course, we'd be delighted." Sarah had an uneasy feeling that her dinner table had just gained a countess. "Countess Ouspenska is an extremely talented artist," she remarked to the company at large, hoping that would more or less explain things.

"How wonderful to be able to create a thing of beauty and a joy forever," said Mrs. Sorpende promptly on cue.

"Also pays off in cash sometimes," replied the talented artist. "Eh, Chuckie?"

Palmerston jumped. "What? Er, yes, I daresay it does. Yes," he went on with more confidence. "I'm sure Bittersohn will agree with me that it might pay off quite handsomely. Especially under certain circumstances." He folded his arms and looked enigmatic.

The countess took no notice of the innuendo. "With me except sometimes, circumstances are stinky. I am not like your good Dolores, who claims she makes one penny do the work of two. Her pennies work not at all. They sit in the piggy bank and rest themselves."

"Dolores Tawne is the salt of the earth," said Brooks with dogged loyalty.

"She is not bad egg," the countess conceded, "only no good for a touch except maybe to the crummy brother."

"I'm afraid she finds Jimmy something of a trial sometimes," Brooks conceded. "Still, he does his job at the palazzo."

"Speaking of the palazzo," Mrs. Sorpende seized her chance to get the conversation back on a decorously cultural level. "I find I am unexpectedly free tomorrow afternoon and I have promised myself the treat of a visit. Oddly enough, I have never been inside the Wilkins Museum."

"Have you not, dear lady?" cried Palmerston. "Then you must grant me the privilege of escorting you in person."

"My God, Chuckie, is life in the old goat yet!"

"Has it ever occurred to you, Countess Ouspenska," Palmerston remarked stiffly, "that some people may find your witticisms a triffle offensive?"

"But of course, Chuckie."

Miss LaValliere giggled again.

Palmerston rose. "I fear I must be getting on. Thank you for a delightful visit, Mrs. Kelling. Bittersohn, I shall expect a progress report from you in my business office Friday morning at nine-fifteen sharp. Mrs. Sorpende, I shall do myself the honor of calling for you in my car at two o'clock tomorrow afternoon if that suits your convenience?"

"Two o'clock will suit me perfectly, Mr. Palmerston."

"Countess Ouspenska," he concluded frostily, "perhaps you will allow me to see you safely back to your studio."

Lydia batted her freight of mascara in surprise, then beamed. "Okay, Chuckie. Is like old times." She blew kisses all around, then swept out on the arm of her fuming escort.

"A most refreshing personality," Mrs. Sorpende observed.

"Who, Palmerston?" snarled Brooks.

"I was thinking of the Countess Ouspenska."

"Oh, Mrs. Kelling, do ask her to dinner soon," bubbled Jennifer LaValliere. "She's a panic! I was devastated when Mr. Palmerston dragged her away. Why was he so nice to her, I wonder, after she'd called him an old goat?"

"Perhaps because he wanted to get her out of here before she called him something else," said Mrs. Gates, who had been enjoying herself a good deal.

"Well, I'm getting out of here, too," grunted Professor Ormsby, and went.

At last Cousin Brooks had Mrs. Sorpende to himself. "Are you going to call him Chuckie?" he beamed in a burst of jealous rage.

"I shouldn't dream of such a thing." Mrs. Sorpende raised one exquisite hand to toy with the satin ribbons at her bodice. "Mr. Palmerston was merely extending a gesture of formal courtesy to a member of this distinguished household. I don't suppose he has any personal interest in me whatever. Do tell me more about the hummingbirds, Mr. Kelling."

"Well," said Brooks, "there's one called the Adorable Coquette."

One by one the others tiptoed out of the library and left them alone with the hummingbirds.

CHAPTER 12

It was well past ten o'clock and Sarah was starting to get ready for bed when she remembered something she'd meant to do about tomorrow's breakfast. She went back to the now deserted kitchen and was attending to her chore when Bittersohn appeared in the doorway from the basement.

"I thought that must be you I heard up here," he said rather diffidently. "I just wanted to thank you for sewing the button on my pajamas."

Sarah flushed. "Oh, that was nothing. I was doing the room and happened to find the button and I – I wonder if we're out of shredded wheat."

"I assumed it must have been Mariposa," he went on, trying to make conversation, which was unlike him, and not showing a very good hand at it, "but when I mentioned it to her she said she can't sew a stitch and Charlie has to do all her mending for her and I knew it couldn't have been Charlie, because he'd already left for work when I popped the button. So I guessed it had to be you."

"Well, it was," Sarah replied inanely. Were they going to stand here making stupid remarks about that button all night? "I must say," she said in an effort to get off that silly subject, "I was surprised when both Mr. Palmerston and your old friend Lydia showed up here tonight. What do you suppose brought them?"

"Hard to say. It couldn't have been prearranged, I shouldn't think. They didn't seem any too happy to see one another."

"I suppose we'll have to assume Mr. Palmerston's idea was to make a little time with Mrs. Sorpende and Lydia thought she'd try her hand with you."

"Why me?"

"She thinks you're magnificent. She keeps telling me so."

"But you don't go along with her."

"Mr. Bittersohn, if you're fishing for compliments, you'll have to choose a time when my mind isn't running on Professor Ormsby's porridge. Have you ever in your life seen anybody eat the way he does?"

"Yes, my uncle Hymie on the night after Yom Kippur. I was wondering, how'd you like to crash the party with me tomorrow?"

"What party? Do you mean invite ourselves to chaperone Mrs. Sorpende and Mr. Palmerston? How could we?"

"We have our methods. Seriously, can you get away from here for a couple of hours?"

"Yes, if I work like a beaver all morning. What should I do?"

"Meet me at the Little Building on the corner of Tremont and Boylston at half-past one. I keep a sort of apology for an office there that I use sometimes for odd jobs." He gave her the room number. "Take the elevator and come straight on up. I'll be inside. Don't expect anything fancy."

"But why not meet somewhere closer to the palazzo?"

"Because we'll need a place to change our clothes."

"From what to what?"

"That depends on what I can scare up at the costume shop."

"Heavens to Betsy! You do know how to make life exciting, Mr. Bittersohn. It's not going to be anything silly like Mickey Mouse ears, is it?"

"Madam, we high-class detectives do not

wear Mickey Mouse ears on secret missions. Unless, of course, it happens to be a Mickey Mouse sort of job, and I'm not at all sure this won't be. Do you have a pair of sandals Mrs. Sorpende wouldn't be apt to recognize?"

"Yes, but they're in sad shape."

"That won't matter. Bring them in a bag. And if Mariposa or anybody asks where you're going, lie. Tell her you're going to see your lawyer about the mortgage lawsuit again."

"I've already milked that man for all he's worth."

"Cheer up, he's probably milking you, too." Bittersohn hesitated a moment, then said rather hastily, "See you tomorrow," and was gone.

He breakfasted early for a change, and was out of the house before Sarah could exchange a word with him about their clandestine rendezvous. Nevertheless she was ascending to the fifth floor of the Little Building that afternoon at half-past one on the dot, sandals in hand. To her surprise, she was met at the door of what proved indeed to be a poky hole of an office by an East Indian, the sort whom she had often seen around a city where foreign students of all races and descriptions abound. His face was bronzed, his short beard and mustache jet black, his hair completely hidden by a turban made from yards and yards of some gauzy pale green material. He wore a cream-colored suit and carried a plastic briefcase.

"I – I beg your pardon," she stammered. "I was expecting – "

"You were expecting maybe Menachem Begin?"

"Mr. Bittersohn! I'd never have known you."

"Such was the intention. Hurry and get into your sari."

"I don't have one."

"Yes, you do and *tempus*, as my new employer would say, *fugit*."

"But I don't know how they go."

"They threw in a diagram." He produced a costumer's box. "See, you put on this blouse thing first, then wrap the curtain thing around you and tuck it in and drag the free end up over your shoulder."

"What if it comes unwrapped?"

"Think positive. I suppose you'd prefer that I step out into the corridor?"

"Considering what I'm going to have to take off to get this rig on, yes."

Bittersohn went out, though he stayed close to the door. She could see his shadow against the ground glass panel. After a minute or so he called, "How are you doing?"

"This blouse is awfully tight," she gasped. "I think it's supposed to button down the front and they haven't made an opening."

"Rise above it."

"That's what I'm doing."

"Want some help?"

"Don't you dare." She'd had to shed her brassiere as well as her slip. At last she managed to cram her round little bosom into the skin-tight bodice, then battled the seemingly endless folds of the sari until she achieved something that bore a remote resemblance to the diagram. "All right now, as long as I don't breathe. You may come in."

Bittersohn reappeared. "Not bad, for a beginner. Where's your lipstick?"

"On my lips, I thought."

"I mean the rest of it. You need a caste mark."

"I need a safety pin."

"Cut the cracks and give me the whatsis."

She handed him her lipstick out of her purse. He tilted up her chin so he could see to make a dot on her forehead between the eyes. His hands felt almost hot and Sarah was surprised to feel them tremble a little.

"There. I made a small one so you're only a half-caste."

"I think I'm totally miscast."

"Funny today, aren't you? Why didn't you put on the sandals?"

"Why didn't you remind me before I got into this cocoon? Now I'm afraid to bend over."

"Where are they? In this bag?" Bittersohn snatched them out, knelt at Sarah's feet, and changed her shoes while she perched on a banged-up desk that was almost the room's only furnishing. "Now the makeup and the wig."

"Makeup? What was the sense of painting that business on my forehead if I have to put makeup over it? And how can I get my arms up to my head in this straitjacket of a blouse?"

"I knew you'd turn out to be a nagger. Hurry it up, we've got to get moving." He crammed the black wig down on her head and flipped its long, thick braid over her shoulder. Then he took a long time trying to poke the little tendrils of brown up off her cheeks. Sarah at last had to finish the job herself.

"There, I'm as ready as I'll ever be. But what about our eyes? Yours are bluish gray and mine are sort of greeny-hazel. Aren't Indian people's always brown?"

"We'll have to keep these on." Bittersohn handed her a pair of cheap sunglasses and put on another pair himself. "And remember, you don't speak a word of English. If anybody speaks to you, just smile and shake your head."

"What if the person is another Indian?"

"You speak a different dialect. Can't you quit grabbing at that sari as if you were afraid it might fall off any second?"

"But I fully expect it to. May I wear my coat or shall I freeze to death in the interests of artistic verisimilitude?"

"Would Mrs. Sorpende recognize the coat?"

"I don't see how she could. It's an old one of my mother's that I've hardly ever worn and she never sees me dressed for the street anyway."

"Then sling it over your shoulders. Here, allow me." Bittersohn bundled Sarah and her assorted garments into the elevator, took them down, and got them a cab. Using what he fondly believed to be a British accent with weird sibilant overtones, he directed the driver to the palace of Madam Wilkins. Then he settled back to develop his role while Sarah huddled in the opposite corner wondering whether to die of embarrassment right away or wait until she was hooted into extinction at Madam's.

She needn't have fretted. Nobody noticed her at all. Mrs. Sorpende had arrived immediately before them. Even the ticket taker at the door was sighing, "Cripes, I didn't think they built 'em like that any more."

Sarah was hurried through the turnstile, then left to string along as best she might. Perhaps Indian wives were expected to trail submissively behind their spouses. Anyway, Bittersohn's efforts to get close to Mrs. Sorpende were unlikely to attract remark either, since every other man in the palazzo was trying to do the same. Hatless women in sensible drip-drys threw angry glances as she sailed up the Grand Staircase with her entourage.

Like Sarah, Mrs. Sorpende had left her coat in the cloakroom as the vast skylights provided an effect of solar heating inside the palazzo. She had on her one and only black daytime dress, a garment that would have been sedate enough if it hadn't happened to fit so divinely. At throat and ears were pearls so discreet as to seem genuine. On her intricately dressed hair perched a whimsy of

165

creamy satin and veiling that would have driven Anatole of France to screaming frenzy. On her hands were gloves of a dazzling whiteness. About her wafted a subtle hint of roses. She was, in a word, sensational.

C. Edwald Palmerston was beaming. He kept patting Mrs. Sorpende's arm to call her attention to one exhibit or another, and orating about the paintings with as much gusto as though he hadn't been informed they were copies. As they reached the Grand Salon and he started gushing about the Romney, a remark of Dolores Tawne's flashed through Sarah's mind: "If you can't tell, what difference does it make?"

So that was how he planned to handle the situation. If Max Bittersohn should fail to recover the stolen paintings, and there were so many of them gone for so long a time that how could he possibly get them all? —then Palmerston would simply go on pretending no robbery had ever happened. The copies would stay where the originals should have been, gathering more layers of dust and varnish that would make it more difficult for even experts to spot the fakery. For so long as Palmerston managed to hold on to his trusteeship, he could see to it that no drastic cleaning or restoration was done. His own face would be saved and another segment of Boston's cultural heritage would be down the drain. Sarah made an involuntary gesture of protest, and her sari came unwrapped.

Luckily all eyes in the vicinity were still on Mrs. Sorpende and there was refuge at hand. It was fortunate that Madam Wilkins had gone in so heavily for sedan chairs. Clutching the elusive silky folds as best she could, Sarah streaked for the nearest, and shut herself inside.

The last occupant of this tiny box on poles might have been some wigged, powdered, and unbathed beauty of Louis XV's reign. The chair smelled as if it hadn't been aired since then. Its small oval windows were green with age and veiled by dust. Sarah crouched gratefully on the narrow seat, as far as she could get from the windows, and undertook repairs.

Desperately she searched the purse she'd remembered to bring with her and produced, wonder of wonders, a small safety pin. After some intricate contortions she managed to get her treacherous draperies fairly smooth and secure. She could leave now. But she didn't. For one thing, her feet were hurting because the nylons she couldn't have borne to take off were making the floppy old sandals skid around. For another, it was rather fun to peek from this secret vantage point at Mrs. Sorpende and her admirers.

Bittersohn was ogling with the best of them and Sarah felt a twinge of annoyance. Ah, now he'd missed his little Indian. He was looking all over the Grand Salon and wasn't seeing her. Yet she herself had a clear view of the entire area, while remaining hidden.

He was getting really puzzled, and beginning to look worried. While the rest drifted on into the Titian Room he began to retrace his steps, walking straight past the sedan chair. Sarah let herself out, noting that the door moved readily without a squeak, and tiptoed up behind him.

"Looking for someone?"

He leaped. If he'd been closer to the balustrade and taken by surprise like this, it might have been possible to shove him over. Especially if he'd been an old man who wasn't too well. Joe Witherspoon must have fallen from just about here.

"For God's sake, where were you?" he whispered fiercely.

All at once Sarah knew exactly where she'd been. She pointed at the sedan chair. "In there. Where the murderer hid before

168

he killed Joe Witherspoon."

Bittersohn walked over, opened the door, stuck his head inside, then ran his forefinger over one of the hinges and held it up filmed with fresh oil. He nodded, wiped his hand on his handkerchief, then hurried Sarah along to rejoin Palmerston's guided tour.

Now came the moment Sarah dreaded most. She stood face to face with her fourth cousin twice removed. Brooks didn't so much as glance at her. He manned his post like a soldier, though the fox of jealousy obviously gnawed at his vitals. Every time Palmerston patted Mrs. Sorpende's white glove, he winced. Every time Palmerston said, "Dear lady," his own lips writhed in silent protest. And every time C. Edwald Palmerston imparted a nugget of information, Brooks contradicted him *sotto voce*, e.g.: "This, dear lady [snarl], is a unique [commonplace] example of fourteenth- [seventeenth-] century French [Flemish] embroidery [tapestry]. It depicts Cupid languishing for Psyche [St. Gambrinus with a hangover]."

As snickers broke out among the group, Palmerston glared at the temporary guard and steered Mrs. Sorpende across to the chapel. But by escaping the knowledgeable

Scylla he ran into a glowering Charybdis in the uninspired shape of Dolores Tawne. For once Mrs. Tawne did not appear overjoyed to see Mr. Palmerston. The gentleman himself turned red as a withered beet, hastily dropped Mrs. Sorpende's arm, and performed an awkward introduction.

"We've met," said Dolores, and went on polishing silver.

"Mrs. Tawne is a veritable bulwark of our museum," Palmerston stammered.

Mrs. Sorpende smiled inscrutably and said she'd been given to understand so. Mrs. Tawne ignored them both. After an uncomfortable moment, the sight-seeing party surged on. But the zest had gone out of the day for Palmerston. His gallantries became furtive and far between. He would have hurried his guest along had Mrs. Sorpende been the kind of lady who allowed herself to be hurried. She continued to move with serene deliberation from one fraudulent work of art to the next.

Sarah was freezing. The sandals were raising blisters on the soles of her feet. That too-tight blouse was a constant misery. Her sari felt loose again and there were no more sedan chairs. She tugged at Bittersohn's elbow from time to time but he sauntered on ogling the imitation Donatellos and the star of the show with impartial admiration. Only after he had watched the gracious lady's ceremonial departure in Palmerston's limousine did he consent to leave.

"If that old letch stays to tea I'll die," Sarah groaned as they were waving with faint hopes at taxis on the Fenway.

"He won't," Bittersohn assured her. "He'll rush straight back to make his peace with Mrs. Tawne. He's scared to death of her, did you notice?"

"Perhaps she reminds him of his mother. Oh, dear, now we have to go back to that office of yours and change again, don't we? And it's getting awfully late. Mariposa will be wondering where I am. I hope to goodness you've accomplished whatever you set out to do."

"I think we learned one or two things, though I'm not altogether sure what. Anyway, I had a feeling it mightn't be too swift to let Mrs. Sorpende go through the palazzo without a bodyguard. And furthermore" — he set his turban at a rakish angle as they at last managed to flag a Checker taxi — "I've always had a hankering to wear one of these things."

CHAPTER 13

Traffic was even worse than they'd expected. By the time they passed the clock on the Arlington Street Church, Sarah was aghast to see that it was almost a quarter to five.

"Mariposa will be having kitten fits!"

"There's a phone in the office. If we ever get there, call her and tell her you've been unavoidably detained. Can't she start dinner without you?"

"Yes, I left everything ready, but what am I going to say? She won't settle for unavoidably detained."

"Then tell her you got caught in a revolving door and have been going around in circles ever since."

"That's exactly how I feel. I hope there's lots of cold cream in that makeup kit you got with the costumes."

"What for?"

"To get this silly greasepaint off with, of course."

"What's wrong with soap and water?"

"Nothing except that it won't work."

"Oh, Jesus!"

Luckily they got to the Little Building soon afterward. It was in the theatrical district, and a nearby drugstore had what they needed. Sarah bought a box of tissues, too, and took a grim satisfaction in making Bittersohn pay for them. Then they went up to the small, depressing office, where their clothes lay sprawled across the desk and chair.

Sarah made her call, told Mariposa she'd been held up at the lawyer's and please to start without her. "I'll be along as soon as I possibly can," she added before Mariposa could express her feelings, and hung up.

Bittersohn was taking an experimental poke at the cold cream and not liking it. "What are we supposed to do with this stuff?"

"Smear it on your face, then wipe it off with tissues. With any luck the makeup will come, too."

"Show me."

Sarah plastered her own cheeks with the white grease, then in exasperation did his, too. They scrubbed and smeared until both were more or less back to their normal hues.

"Now we must change. Will you go first, or shall I?"

"Why don't we just turn our backs and be ladies and gentlemen?"

"All right, it is getting awfully late." And Cousin Mabel was quite some distance away. Sarah flipped the dirty venetian blinds shut, retreated behind the desk to give some semblance of privacy, and unwrapped her sari. Then came the problem of getting out of that blouse, and there she stuck, literally. She managed to get the bottom up just far enough to immobilize her shoulder joints. Her arms were useless. She squirmed, she struggled. Nothing would budge. At last she gasped, "You'll have to help me."

"My God, how did you ever get into this thing in the first place?" Bittersohn tugged with all his might. The blouse came off, and there was Sarah.

That did it, of course. She'd known this was going to happen sooner or later. She hadn't expected it to happen in a grimy office on the Windy Corner with Bittersohn in his undershirt and herself in nothing but a pair of panty hose and both their faces greasy with cheap cold cream. And Mr. Porter-Smith, like as not, already on his way to the library in his wine-colored tuxedo with the burgundy satin lapels expecting her to be there to pour his sherry. It shouldn't be happening like this. It shouldn't be happening at all with dear, darling Alexander only five months dead. Yet she'd wanted it to happen. She wanted it to go on happening until everything had happened that could happen, but she mustn't let it. She pulled away and began putting on her clothes.

"I'm sorry," said Bittersohn huskily. "That was unpardonable of me."

"I know," she answered with her head turned away. "That's why I kept slapping your face and telling you to stop. Oh, Max, I — " She had her blouse and skirt on now. Maybe it would be all right to go back into his arms, just for a moment. "Could you — bear with me a little while? Give me a chance to get my feet under me?"

"Then what?" he murmured into the back of her neck.

"Then we'll have to see what develops, won't we?" She could hear her voice shaking. So was her body. "You may decide you'd rather not be bothered."

"Sarah, for God's sake! Do you know what it's like for me, lying alone down there in the basement and knowing you're upstairs in that double bed by yourself? It's getting so I have to chain myself to the bedposts."

"Well, it's no picnic for me either, if you want to know. Furthermore, you don't have any bedposts, so don't be melodramatic. Come on, get dressed and let's go home before Charles evicts us both for lack of couth."

"Jesus, you're a hard woman." Yet Bittersohn was smiling as they left the office.

They walked back across the Common. It was silly to take a cab for so short a distance, and pleasant for a weary young woman to hang on the arm of a gallant gentleman who kept assisting her over the curbstones and potholes even when there weren't any. They went in the back way because it would have been silly to risk Mrs. Sorpende's seeing them together and perhaps remembering something they didn't want her to know. The little dark entry where the trash cans were kept happened to be a safe though unromantic nook for a landlady to get kissed in by a boarder without being caught. It would have been silly to pass up the chance.

What with avoiding all that silliness, it was perilously close to dinnertime when Sarah rushed into the kitchen panting. "Mariposa, I'm so sorry. Is everything all right?"

"Comin' along just fine, honey. Where you been all this time?"

"I told you, at the lawyer's office."

"Yeah, that's what you told me. El señor Max, he been at the lawyer's office, too?"

"Of course not! We simply happened to run into one another."

"Must have been some collision!"

"I've got to change."

Sarah might have known Mariposa would see them coming in the back way together and draw the obvious conclusion as to why it took her so long to get upstairs. When she'd got to her room and caught a glimpse of her smudged face and disordered garments in the mirror, she decided she wouldn't have believed the story about the lawyer, either. Well, Mariposa was a fine one to talk.

She did a fast clean-up and threw on an indestructible dinner dress of black crepe that had seen her mother through many a season before Sarah fell heir to it. If she was subconsciously trying to remind herself that she was still a widow mourning her beloved husband she couldn't be succeeding any too well. She'd no sooner got down to the library than Mrs. Gates commented, "Mrs. Kelling, you look positively radiant tonight. May one hope that your meeting was successful?"

"We've made some progress, at any rate," said Sarah, trying not to look at Mr. Bittersohn and sensing that he was trying not to look at her. "Mrs. Sorpende, thank you so much for taking my place. You do it so much better than I. Charles, have I time for a quick sherry before dinner?"

"You have five minutes, madam." Charles was clearly miffed at not having been able to play to a full house during the past hour.

Sarah took the drink anyway. She felt the need. "How was your trip to the Madam's, Mrs. Sorpende?"

"Highly educational." Mrs. Sorpende appeared radiant, too. Surely she hadn't fallen for C. Edwald? How could she even tolerate the man, unless she was taking into consideration his wealth, social position, and availability? Mrs. Palmerston had died ages ago of sheer exasperation, or so Anora Protheroe claimed. "To be sure," Mrs. Sorpende went on, "there were many points on which I should require a great deal of instruction. Do you think it would be in order for me to ask your cousin Mr. Brooks Kelling to elucidate?"

"I think it would be quite in order. I'm sure Brooks knows lots more than Mr. Palmerston." Sarah caught Charles's eye and nodded. "Shall we go in?"

She didn't dare let Mr. Bittersohn sit beside her tonight, so she used Mrs. Gates and Mr. Porter-Smith for buffers. He in retaliation turned his attention to Miss LaValliere. Mrs. Sorpende got into a conversation about Madam Wilkins with Mrs. Gates, who could well remember the eccentric millionairess. Professor Ormsby, as usual, concentrated on eating everything within sight. That left Sarah to Eugene Porter-Smith and she was content that it should be so. One didn't have to converse with Mr. Porter-Smith, one had only to nod at regular intervals and let one's mind wander whither it listed. Sarah didn't dare let hers wander to what had happened in Bittersohn's office, so she concentrated on the sedan chair.

Why would Witherspoon's killer have had to hide in it? If he was one of the other guards, he could have strolled over pretending to look at the clock as Dolores Tawne suggested, commit a minor offense as Nick Fieringer claimed they did, or simply to stretch his legs and chat a moment. Sarah didn't believe for a moment that every single one of the guards, except probably the timid Melanson, was all that punctilious about never leaving his station when there was a lull in the flow of visitors.

If the killer was somebody Witherspoon didn't know, he or she could have posed as a casual visitor, perhaps call the guard over to ask a question or start to do a spot of damage so that Witherspoon would rush out from the Titian Room to stop him. But if it was somebody who knew Joe Witherspoon and wasn't supposed to be in the palazzo at that time, such as Mr. Fitzroy, the superintendent, who was supposed to be taking the day off — she realized she'd forgotten to nod at the right time and Mr. Porter-Smith was looking put out.

"Do go on," she begged. "You have such a graphic way of explaining things." Actually she hadn't the least notion of what he'd been talking about but Mr. Porter-Smith was quite ready to take her urging at face value and let her get back to her ponderings.

Who else might have turned up when he shouldn't have? Dolores Tawne? No, she appeared to have carte blanche to come and go as she pleased. Dolores's brother Jimmy? He was said to have been sick, but was he? Might he have pretended to stay away in order to give himself an alibi? Then how would he have got up that all too open

Grand Staircase without being seen?

Unless he'd stayed inside the museum all the previous night. But he couldn't have stayed the following night, too, because the museum was searched. Had he gone back inside the chair and trusted to luck he'd be overlooked in the confusion that was sure to follow Witherspoon's death? Disguised himself as an Indian? Sarah thought she'd better not think too much about disguises.

That act of Brown's with the chapel silver might well have been prearranged to draw attention away from the Grand Salon so that somebody who was in fact hidden in the sedan chair so conveniently near the stairway would have a chance to get away while Brown was pretending to revive and drawing attention to the imaginary assault.

Brown's being murdered afterward would make sense in that context. If you'd played a part in somebody's murder plot, that somebody might decide you weren't safe to be left alive, especially if you were lazy, untrustworthy, and inclined to nip on the job. Unlikely as he sounded from the little she'd heard of him, Sarah thought Jimmy Agnew couldn't be counted out, if only because his station was so convenient to Witherspoon's and because he was used to doing what he was told to do by his sister, the ubiquitous handywoman.

And who else? Nick Fieringer? Sarah caught her breath. Theoretically Nick should have been down on the second floor in the Tintoretto Room during the concert, waiting there alone until the performers had finished their playing and taken their bows and gone back there for the modest reception that would follow. But had he? Nobody was apt to have been checking on him, and even during the aftermath of the concert he could have absented himself and not been greatly missed.

She'd noticed on the one or two other occasions when she'd been to performances Fieringer arranged that he had a trick of self-effacement he could turn on and off. It was part of his "good old Nick, always ready to take a back seat and let his performers have all the credit" routine. He could have nipped down that one flight of stairs even while she and Max were talking to Brooks over under the Romney, where their view of the stairs would have been obscured by those sedan chairs scattered about the balcony. Then he'd simply have mingled with the guests, pretending he'd been in the Tintoretto Room all the time.

If anybody had happened to see him coming from the third floor, he could have used that obscene excuse of having gone up to the source of the fountain to relieve himself. Since the top basin was on the far side of the courtyard from the staircase, almost directly opposite where Joe Witherspoon had gone over the balustrade, he could even have claimed he'd seen the guard throw himself over, only he hadn't had to perjure himself because he'd got away with it. Assuming of course that she wasn't maligning an innocent man.

The performers themselves were assuredly innocent. They'd been on public view all the time. But what about those tacky friends of Bernie the pianist? According to Lydia Ouspenska they were all petty thieves to begin with. Bengo painted genuine old masterpieces, Lupe was an operator; there was no telling what the rest might be up to. Sarah could believe almost anything of that lot but why should they have hidden in the sedan chair? It was unlikely Witherspoon would have known any of them, and they all looked much alike anyway.

Except Lydia Ouspenska. The countess would stand out anywhere. Since she knew Dolores Tawne and had been Palmerston's mistress it was more than likely she'd visited the palazzo on various occasions, and Witherspoon had been there since the beginning of time. He'd surely have recognized Lydia if she'd let him see her, and that sedan chair was precisely the sort of exotic hiding place that would appeal to her sense of drama.

Sarah didn't want it to be Lydia. Enough of this. She gave Mr. Porter-Smith a final nod, turned him over to Miss LaValliere, and started talking to Mrs. Gates about Seiji Ozawa.

CHAPTER 14

This happened to be one of those evenings when everybody was going somewhere. Mrs. Gates had a spare ticket to Symphony and asked Mrs. Sorpende to go with her. Professor Ormsby had a faculty meeting. Miss LaValliere's grandmother on Mount Vernon Street was giving a reception and had commanded Jennifer to show up with a few presentable young men, so Mr. Porter-Smith was obliging with his august self and a couple of his underlings from the accounting office. Mariposa and Charles had plans of their own, no doubt.

That left Sarah alone with Max Bittersohn. She was wondering if it would be madness to invite him up to her private sitting room and he was no doubt wondering whether she'd be mad enough to ask him, when the doorbell rang. "I'll get it," Sarah said, rather glad of an excuse to break the tension.

"No, I will. I don't want you answering doors after dark." The dominant male strode to the hallway. A moment later Sarah heard him say, "Advance and give the password."

"Wilkins, I expect," came Brooks Kelling's voice. "Are you receiving tonight?"

"Sure. My esteemed landlady and I were just wondering where we could find a third for pinochle. What's up?"

"First, I thought you'd be interested to know that Palmerston called a meeting of the guards this morning, myself included, and informed us he's arranged with an outside expert to make an appraisal of the paintings in the museum."

"I was wondering when he'd think of that. Who's he getting, do you know?"

"A Spaniard connected with the Prado, I believe. His name is Dr. Aguinaldo Ruy Lopez."

"Do tell. When's he supposed to be coming?"

"Tomorrow no less. Palmerston says he's flying Ruy Lopez in from Barcelona at his own expense."

"I thought the Prado was in Madrid," said Sarah.

"It is. Please don't inject trivia. As I was about to say, Palmerston told us that after

186

the recent disturbing events, as he so genteelly alluded to them, he'd decided on the appraisal as a routine formality. He said it was a decision of the board of trustees, which is a lot of rot. They haven't held a meeting in fifteen years."

"Was Mrs. Tawne at your meeting?"

"Of course."

"What did she think of Palmerston's idea?"

"She was all for it. Afterward she tried to make us believe she was the one who'd suggested it in the first place."

"After the meeting?"

"No, later. After he'd flaunted his conquest."

"Brooks, do quit curling your lip like that," cried Sarah. "Surely you can't think an intelligent woman like Mrs. Sorpende could have been taken in by that old gasbag? She was only being civil to him because she didn't want to embarrass me. Since he made the offer in my house, she thought it her duty to be gracious and accept."

"Oh? Does she look upon me as a duty, too?"

"Don't be silly. She considers you a pleasure and a privilege. And for your information she's gone to Symphony with Mrs. Gates tonight, so you needn't flash those big

187

green eyes. She'll be desolate when she finds she's missed you. She was asking me at dinner if I thought she could get you to explain some things about the Madam's because Palmerston's such an idiot she couldn't understand what he was trying to say half the time."

"Was she indeed?"

"Well, she's too much of a lady to come straight out and say so, but that was the clear implication. Wasn't it, M-Mr. Bittersohn?"

"I never heard anything more clearly not said. Getting back to this Ruy Lopez, Kelling, have you any idea when he's due to arrive?"

"Nine o'clock in the morning. Time and a half for the extra hour since we don't usually open to the public till ten. We were all pathetically grateful for this unexpected largesse."

"No doubt. How might one get a look at Ruy Lopez?"

"One might lurk in the shrubbery."

"One might get run in as a suspicious character. Any more bright ideas?"

"Would you be content with a photograph?"

"Sure, but what makes you think he'd pose for you?"

"Naturally he wouldn't know the pictures were being taken."

"I see. You'd have a miniature camera concealed in your tiepin."

"No, my belt buckle. I got the idea from a Dick Tracy cartoon and worked out the details myself. I use it mostly for photographing ospreys' nests and so forth. It leaves both hands free to hang on with when I'm in a high tree or dangling on a rope over a precipice. After all, I'm not so young as I used to be."

Bittersohn grinned. "You'll never get me to believe that. Are you sure he won't spot the camera?"

"You didn't." Brooks produced two tiny but embarrassingly good prints. One showed Bittersohn in his turban gazing at Mrs. Sorpende's rear elevation with a disgusting leer on his temporarily swarthy face. The second was of Sarah clutching her disintegrating sari with one hand and rubbing a blistered foot with the other.

"My God! Do you think Palmerston recognized us, too?"

"I'm sure he didn't. You have to remember, Bittersohn, that I'm a highly trained observer. Once you've learned to identify thirty or forty different warblers on the wing you're unlikely to be put off by a dot of lipstick on the forehead of your own fourth cousin twice removed. Actually your disguises were very good, although I think Sarah would have been more comfortable in a looser bodice. As a matter of academic curiosity, Sarah, how did you ever get in and out of that garment?"

"With great difficulty," she replied demurely. "What else did you have to tell us, Brooks?"

"Well, for another thing, the natives are restless. None of the guards believes Brown killed himself and they're beginning to wonder about Witherspoon. There's a lot of talk. Not to Dolores, of course."

"Because she carries tales to Palmerston?"

"Mainly because they don't like her. I've always considered Dolores the salt of the earth, but now that I'm in close daily contact with her I find she tends to be something of a bully, if one can apply that epithet to a woman, as I suppose one can nowadays. For instance, she laid Melanson out this morning for being a rabbit, which was both unkind and zoologically inaccurate."

"Has she expressed any theories about Brown and Witherspoon?" asked Bittersohn.

"She's convinced that both deaths were

accidental, or says she is. She claims Brown tried to fake a suicide for the same reason he rigged that stupid robbery scene in the chapel, as a childish bid for attention. She claims a man who drank things like bay rum and vanilla extract probably figured a little paint remover wouldn't hurt him. One has to admit that's a credible hypothesis. She also claims Brown led Jimmy astray, however, and that's arrant hogwash."

"What does Jimmy himself say?"

"Nothing worth repeating. Jimmy never has a thought in his head that isn't directly concerned with getting a drink."

"Was he really sick last Sunday?" Sarah asked.

"I presume so because he had to pay me to substitute for him out of his own pocket, or his sister's more likely. Jimmy had already used up his annual sick leave nursing hangovers. What makes you think he wasn't?"

"I was just thinking." She explained what she'd been thinking. "Does that make any sense to you? Would it be possible, for instance, for Jimmy Agnew to have reached the third floor and got out again without being spotted on a day when he was sup-posed to be absent?"

Brooks thought the matter over. "I can't say it's impossible," he said at last. "For one thing, one gets so used to seeing a guard in uniform that even his ordinary outdoor clothing might constitute a sufficient disguise. Then you have to consider the small number of guards on duty in relation to the amount of clutter we're supposed to be able to see around. It would not be hard for a person to get into that sedan chair without being seen, just as you did this afternoon even though a considerable number of people were standing not far away. As to what might have drawn Joe Witherspoon away from the Titian Room, I'm afraid the crass suggestion made by Mr. Fieringer is not wholly unreasonable. Joe's kidneys were a source of vulgar ribaldry around the locker room. The person in the sedan chair would only have to lie low and wait for the opportune moment, dump Joe as he was going along the balcony, then jump back in again and choose an opportune moment to escape. Brown's trick in the chapel, as you suggest, might have been deliberately planned to provide that moment. Alternatively, the murderer might have stayed in the chair till everybody else had cleared out, then simply left at his leisure.

There's only one watchman at night. Anybody with even a vague knowledge of the layout would be able to dodge him easily enough. I don't know about those other people you mention, but surely anybody who has access to the palazzo during the off hours, such as Dolores or Mr. Fitzroy, or Mr. Palmerston – "

"I'd root for Mr. Palmerston on general principles," said Sarah, "except that he's far more interested in avoiding scandals at the Madam's than causing them. Besides –"

"Besides what?"

"I'm afraid Mr. Bittersohn isn't going to like this idea."

Mr. Bittersohn didn't. When she mentioned Nick Fieringer, he shook his handsome head. "I can't buy that. Nick was with the musicians. Ask Bernie. Ask that kid who thinks she's a cellist. Both of whom would lie their heads off for the great impresario, no doubt. Why did you have to think of Nick?"

"I'm sorry. Maybe you can find witnesses who saw him during the whole performance. Unbiased ones, I mean."

"Who's unbiased? Nick is everybody's pal. If they didn't see him for a while, they'd think he was out packing up the music or something. How did I get myself into this, anyway? I think I'll give up my sordid profession and get Mrs. Sorpende to teach me Belgian lacework instead."

"Is Mrs. Sorpende a lacemaker?" Cousin Brooks perked up. "I designed an improved butterfly net years ago, but could never find anybody able to make a trial model for me."

"I'm sure she'd be thrilled to pieces if you asked her," said Sarah. "Why don't you come to dinner again tomorrow night and bring your plans?"

"Splendid suggestion. Thank you, Sarah." And off he bounded, happy as a bunny in a clover field.

Sarah yawned. "What a day this has been! I'd better put the porridge to soak and go to bed."

"Need any help?" Bittersohn asked hopefully as he followed her out to the kitchen.

"At what?"

She laughed and blushed. He bent and kissed her gently on the mouth. It was too much like that last night in the kitchen at Ireson's Landing, the one night of her seven-year marriage when she and Alexander had been truly happy together. She buried her face in Bittersohn's shirt front and burst into tears.

"For God's sake, Sarah!" He was talking

through clenched teeth. "Is this what it's going to be like every time?"

She wiped her eyes and tilted her head back to look him full in the face. "Now, you listen to me, Max Bittersohn. I'm going to be twenty-seven years old next month and Alexander would have been fifty-one in September. We never had a marriage at all, in the usual sense of the word. But we did love each other and — and what sort of woman would I be to you if I could just stick him off somewhere like a book I'd finished reading and never think of him again? I'm not going to pretend I don't want you, because I do. If you can't wait till I'm ready, then that's my tough luck. But there's no sense in your trying to force the issue because I'm doing the best I can and I can't do any better."

Bittersohn kissed her again, even more gently than before. "I'll be around, Sarah. Let me know when you're ready, okay?"

She managed to smile. "I'll more or less have to, shan't I? Good night, Max. Keep your buttons on."

CHAPTER 15

Knowing where they stood with one another made the situation between Sarah and Max Bittersohn easier in some ways, harder in others. For instance, it was difficult to maintain a serene and decorous mien in front of Mrs. Gates and Mrs. Sorpende when one was getting pinched in a sensitive place and Mariposa was being ever so obvious about not noticing what was going on behind one's chair. Life was never like this in the old days, when Alexander would have been letting himself be browbeaten by Aunt Caroline and Edith would have been making a great to-do about clearing away because she was so grievously overworked. One could adjust to change. One simply gave one's lovesick swain a mild kick on the ankle and went about one's daily tasks.

If one rushed to be downstairs early, dressed in one's best, to meet one's boarders for sherry, one was only making up for one's dereliction of the previous evening. If one's first arrival happened to be Cousin Brooks, one merely tried not to look disappointed.

"Hi, Sarah, where is everybody?" was his greeting.

"Getting dressed for dinner, mostly. They should start trickling down pretty soon. Were you looking for somebody special?"

"Yes, Bittersohn. I have his picture."

"So soon? Mariposa, would you mind — "

But Mariposa didn't have to mind. Bittersohn, usually the last one to arrive, came charging in. "I thought I heard the patter of little feet. How did you make out, Kelling?"

"Rather successfully, I think." Brooks passed over the tiny squares of paper.

Bittersohn took a look and went into convulsions. When he could speak, he passed the snapshots over to Sarah. "Get a load of Palmerston's expert!"

"It can't be!"

"Would your own fourth cousin's belt buckle lie to you?" said Bittersohn. "It's Lupe all right. Look at those weaselly little eyes, and the beard." In spite of the ambassadorial garb and a strange appearance of having bathed and visited a barber, the man in the pictures was indubitably their recent acquaintance from Brookline Village. "I don't know how he dealt this hand, but maybe I'll find out later. I'm planning to see him, you know."

"Oh yes, this was the night he's to have Rembrandt's cat ready. Do you think he will?"

"Sure. He's probably authenticating the cat right now. That, madam, is an operator."

Charles, who had just got home from the plastics factory and made his quick change into his buttling garb, came rushing through the hall to answer the doorbell. A moment later he coughed sadly at the library door. "Mr. Palmerston is here, madam. Will he be staying to dinner?"

"He will not," said Sarah. "You may as well show him in. Mr. Bittersohn, shall Brooks and I leave?"

"No, stick around. This should be interesting."

Palmerston bustled in behind Charles. "Well, Bittersohn, I'm happy to inform you that the situation is under control."

"Great," said Bittersohn.

"You may well say so. I had the inspired thought of getting your — er — friend's findings verified by a genuine expert. I selected Dr. Aguinaldo Ruy Lopez who, as you must of course know, is one of Europe's leading authorities on pre- and post-Renaissance paintings."

"How about during?" said Bittersohn.

Palmerston pretended not to hear. "I had Dr. Ruy Lopez flown to Boston at my own expense. He visited the Wilkins Museum first thing this morning and spent much of the day examining the paintings you questioned. He informs me on the basis of his own personal knowledge" – Palmerston waggled a bony forefinger to emphasize every word – "his – own – personal – knowledge, mind you, that your appraisal was wrong in almost every case."

"Was the curator from the Metropolitan wrong, too?"

"There is," said Palmerston with aristocratic hauteur, "such a thing as professional jealousy. I make no such accusation. The charitable assumption is that you and your – er – associates, whoever they may be, were misled by the possibility that very old copies of the paintings may exist, or even that modern copies may conceivably have been made and sold as originals. Dr. Ruy Lopez informs me that this sort of thing is occasionally done by – er – unscrupulous people."

"Dr. Ruy Lopez would certainly know. May I ask how you happened to think of calling him in?"

"As a matter of fact, I did not think of him. My first inclination was to approach someone known to me personally. Upon sober reflection, however, I deemed it wiser to employ an expert who had no connection with any local museum and might therefore be relied upon to give a totally – er – non-parochial opinion. I then conferred with various persons whose opinions I respect. Several names were put forth and it was determined that Dr. Ruy Lopez would be the best man for the job. A transatlantic telephone call and a bit of string-pulling with one of the larger airlines, and the thing was done." He favored them with a smirk of self-congratulation.

"I suppose it was Mrs. Tawne who suggested Dr. Ruy Lopez," Sarah observed innocently.

"No, as a matter of fact it was our musical director, Mr. Nicholas Fieringer."

Bittersohn looked a bit sick.

"Dr. Ruy Lopez has in fact given me the names of three paintings he believes to be spurious." Palmerston dragged out a gold-tooled leather notebook bristling with slips of paper. "Ah, yes, here it is. These, he tells me, are post-Renaissance copies about which he believes Mrs. Wilkins must have been duped at the time of purchase."

"And you're willing to take his word against the opinions of three others?"

"I fail to see why I should not. The unbiased opinion of an eminent scholar appears to bear sufficient weight to offset the casual speculations of — er — possible sensation seekers. Therefore I have decided to proceed no further. This whole affair, sir, was a mare's nest."

"The hell it was."

"Mr. Bittersohn, if you persist in your efforts to pursue an investigation, I shall be forced to give credence to a suspicion that has been voiced to me but that I have hitherto been reluctant to entertain." Palmerston puffed out his cheeks and glared down his nose. "It is that you have seized upon the chance to exploit our recent tragedies with the object of mulcting the Wilkins Museum of a substantial fee."

Bittersohn half rose from his chair.

"But of course," Palmerston went on quickly, "such behavior would be unthinkable in a person of your — er — doubtless merited professional standing. So I think the best plan at this juncture will be for us to agree quietly among ourselves that a mistake has been made and part with no hard feelings on either side. You must feel free, of course, to submit a bill to me personally for whatever services you may have rendered in good faith, even though they turned out to be — er — unnecessary."

"Good night, Mr. Palmerston," said Bittersohn quietly.

Sarah touched the bell. "Charles, show Mr. Palmerston out."

"I trust you understand my position, Mrs. Kelling." The head trustee twisted his features into a placatory simper. "I should not wish to lose your good opinion of me."

"My opinion of you has not changed, Mr. Palmerston. Good night."

"Perhaps you will convey my respects to Mrs. Sorpende?"

Sarah did not answer. Charles stood waiting. Palmerston left.

"Charles," said Sarah after the door had closed, "if that man ever tries to set foot in this house again, you're to pour boiling oil on his head."

"It will be my pleasure, madam. May I offer you sherry?"

"By all means."

Brooks raised his glass. "Confusion to our enemy!"

"I'll drink to that," said Sarah. "I hope he develops a carbuncle where it hurts most."

"I hope he chokes," snarled Bittersohn, "when I make him eat his words."

They ate, drank, and were merry to show they didn't care. After dinner Bittersohn went downstairs to equip himself for the expedition to Brookline Village. Rather alarmed, Sarah made an excuse about something in the laundry room and followed him.

"Max, you're not going to see that Lupe now, are you?"

"Sure, why not?"

"But suppose he's found out who you really are?"

"Big deal. I've been fired from the case, remember?"

"You don't intend to drop it, then?"

"How can I? Don't you think Palmerston is going to start dropping hints around town about Bittersohn the phony? You heard him offer me a bribe. He'll be saying I can be bought. If my reputation for honesty and reliability gets cut down, I'll be lucky to wind up teaching art history at Miss Foofeldinker's finishing school for thirty bucks a week. Damn it, Sarah" — he put his arms around her and rested his cheek on her soft hair — "you wouldn't want that to happen, would you?"

"Having you cooped up in a classroom with a lot of Miss LaVallieres twitching their behinds at you? I should say not! All right, Max, give me five minutes to change."

"You're not coming, *fischele*. Go be a nice landlady."

Sarah knew better than to insist. She rejoined her boarders and found the library a scene of infant gaiety. Cousin Brooks was demonstrating how he ran a birthday party. He was impersonating a barn owl. Mrs. Sorpende was acting with verve the part of a field mouse about to be caught. Professor Ormsby was the barn, Miss LaValliere the weather vane, Mrs. Gates the cow in the stall, and Mr. Porter-Smith a badger for some reason Sarah couldn't grasp.

There was a great deal of giggling and scuttling about, then Cousin Brooks pounced on Mrs. Sorpende and announced that the owl had caught the field mouse, the badger must return to its hole beside the barn and usually about now they served the ice cream and birthday cake. He whipped a handful of paper hats out of his pocket and passed them around. They all put on the hats and sang, "Happy birthday to you."

Charles, caught up in the general merriment, entered with a tray of liqueurs. Mrs. Sorpende insisted on lighting a candle for Brooks to blow out before he was allowed to sip his crème de menthe. It was all so charmingly silly that Sarah almost forgot to worry about Max until the doorbell rang.

Charles parked his tray on the Chippendale lowboy and went to see who was there. He came back and murmured to Sarah, "Mr. Fieringer would like to see you, madam."

"Heavens, don't let him in here." The entire group, wearing their paper hats, were now playing ring-around-a-rosy with Mrs. Gates as the rosy since she was too old and frail to go cavorting about like the rest. "Take him up to the studio. I'll see him there."

Forgetting to take off her paper hat, she went to greet the impresario. Fieringer was looking unhappy, and Sarah knew he expected her to be furious with him about Bittersohn's getting fired. She was, now that she remembered. Too late, she also remembered the paper hat. Snatching it off, she demanded, "Is this a friendly visit, Mr. Fieringer, or did you come to be offensive like your boss?"

"I came to see is my old friend Maxie

205

mad at me," he replied frankly.

"I am not in a position to answer for Mr. Bittersohn."

"Beautiful lady, what could I do? Palmerston comes to me with a problem. Everybody brings problems to old Nick. Palmerston says to me, 'Who can I get?' I say Bittersohn is best. He says, 'Bittersohn is Harvard, I am Yale Class of '32, how can I trust Bittersohn?'"

"Are you sure that's what he said, Mr. Fieringer? In the first place, Mr. Bittersohn went to Boston University."

"So all right it's Palmerston went to Harvard and BU he doesn't trust. I'm an old man, I get confused. And Bill Jones — "

"Oh, you know Bill Jones?"

"I tell you, lady. I know everybody. I see Bill Jones at the Madam's poking around, I know Maxie must have sent him. Bill Jones is from stolen originals an expert, naturally he tells Maxie stolen originals, not somebody passing fakes."

"Are you implying that Bill Jones lied?"

"Bill Jones lied?" Nick was horrified. "Bill couldn't lie about nothing. Not to save his own mother Bill couldn't lie. That's why he gets along so good with crooks. I don't say Bill lied, only he made a mistake."

"And Mr. Bittersohn and that curator from the Metropolitan made a mistake, too? A mistake that must run into heaven knows how many million dollars? That was some mistake, wasn't it?"

"Exactly." Fieringer smiled broadly and wiped his forehead. "Is too big a problem to trust to one expert. Better we get somebody international is what Palmerston says."

"I'd like to know who's more international than Mr. Bittersohn. We never know whether he's going to call up from Brussels or Bangkok to say he'll be late for dinner."

Fieringer perspired yet more freely. "Beautiful lady, all I know is Palmerston is my boss. He asks me who in the world is best. I tell him after Bittersohn, Ruy Lopez is best. 'So we get Ruy Lopez,' he says. Believe me, I had nothing more to do with it than that."

"How did you happen to know about Dr. Ruy Lopez?"

"I hear the name from somebody. Everybody tells old Nick everything. I tell Palmerston, he takes it from there."

"Oh, then you didn't make the contact yourself?"

"Me? If it's a bassoon player maybe Palmerston lets me make the contact. In so important a matter you think he trusts only the word of old Nick Fieringer? He checks with the Art Museum naturally, he checks maybe at the Fogg, the Busch-Reisinger, how do I know where else? They say get Ruy Lopez, he gets Ruy Lopez."

"Oh, then quite a number of people would have known what he was intending to do?"

"But of course. With Palmerston is always the fanfare of trumpets, the beating of drums."

And after all that trouble, he'd come up with a Lupe. "How remarkable," said Sarah.

CHAPTER 16

What was also remarkable was the way Fieringer was sweating. His yellowish fat face shone like a full moon. A wet ball of handkerchief was clenched in his fist. Immense dark crescents were spreading under the armpits of his gray suit coat. In this prim little room with its white paint and figured chintz he was monstrous. Sarah wished desperately that he'd leave, yet she knew she would have to keep him there until Max Bittersohn returned.

"Do let me offer you something to drink," she urged. "Would you care for coffee? A liqueur? Cold beer?"

"Beer would be fine." He licked his lips. It was obvious that old Nick wasn't enjoying this visit any more than Sarah was, but he had no intention of leaving without seeing Bittersohn. Why? Did he know who the alleged Ruy Lopez who'd appeared at the Madam's really was, and did he want to find out if Bittersohn knew, too? Had Palmerston sent him to make sure the case would really be dropped? Was it simply that this fat old man felt a need to make peace? Could he not bear to have anybody angry with him?

As this musical Falstaff pulled noisily at the beer Charles brought, Sarah thought what a remarkably unsavory person he was to be near. He was clean enough as far as that went, but he was so appallingly gross! And there was that overdone effusiveness, with the tension rasping underneath enough to set one's teeth on edge. She began to wonder if all those people really liked Nick all that much. Everyone's pal might be nobody's friend. And he'd know. What a ghastly life it must be for a sensitive man.

"Let me have Charles bring up some fresh beer for you."

Now she was doing what others must do. People would always be overly affable with Nick Fieringer because they'd always be ashamed of what they were feeling toward him. They'd know it was unfair to loathe a man just because he was such a mess but how did one control an instinctive revulsion? Didn't he ever want to hit back? Was that what he'd done at the Madam's?

If Nicholas Fieringer's revenge on Boston

had taken the form of a multimillion-dollar art robbery, what had he done with the proceeds? He was perpetually, notoriously hard up. Was the poverty a bluff, like his hearty good-fellowship? Had he got the money salted away somewhere ready for him to go off and enjoy while he had his private laugh at the fools who'd despised him and let him rob them blind? Or had he spent it on buying a reputation for being a good guy? Sponges like Bernie, leeches like that Lupe creature could get through fortunes in no time flat, as Sarah knew to her sorrow. They'd throw it away on drugs or gambling or whatever caught their fancies and come dancing back to good old Nick for more. To her surprise, Sarah felt tears rolling down her cheeks.

Fieringer could hardly have helped noticing. "What's wrong, beautiful lady? Tell old Nick. Everybody brings their troubles to Nick."

She brushed a hand over her face. "It's just that you reminded me for a moment of my husband. I suppose you know what happened to him. It wasn't very long ago, you know, and I still haven't quite — "

Whatever was possessing her to go on like that? How could any two people on earth have been less alike than this fat, sweating, vulgar hulk and the incredibly handsome, fastidious aristocrat she'd loved and lost? Yet there had been that same tension under Alexander's eternal self-possession, that same need to be the kind father figure on whom the whole Kelling clan dumped their problems, and that same cruel exploitation, although thank God he never found it out. She had often resented him for being the way he was, and felt ashamed of herself and tried to make up for it by being extra sweet just as she was doing now with Nick Fieringer. And Nick was taking it in the way most dreadful to her, as she ought to have known he would.

"Believe me, it is a great honor what you say. I will cherish always in my heart the memory. Only when I die will be no beautiful woman to weep for me." He was grimacing like somebody in an ad for denture cleaners. It was obscene.

"I'm sure that isn't so," she replied lamely. How in God's name did one talk to a man like this without vomiting? One might at least try to get away from personalities. "I've often wondered," she ventured, "exactly what an impresario does."

Fieringer told her. It took forever. In the midst of his monologue he excused himself with a mixture of playfulness and embarrassment to go to the bathroom. Was there nothing the man could do without giving it the flavor of a dirty joke? She longed for him to go away, for Bittersohn to come back, for the house to catch fire. She'd given Charles pointed orders to show Mr. Bittersohn up here the second he set foot in the house. At last, at very long last, he came.

"How are you, Nick? Sorry to keep you waiting so long. Did Mrs. Kelling offer you anything to drink?" His heartiness was as false as Fieringer's although he was managing it more gracefully.

Sarah was frantic to get him alone and find out what had happened at Lupe's but no relief was in sight. First the impresario had to tell his dear friend Maxie what a wonderful time he'd been having with the beautiful landlady in a way that made Sarah want to go and take a long, hot shower. Then he had to make his speech about Palmerston and Ruy Lopez. The version he gave Max didn't jibe any too well with the story he'd told her, Sarah noted. How could the man succeed at grand larceny over a long span of years if he couldn't manage to keep his lies straight for a single evening? Sarah heaved a silent sigh and rang for more beer.

"By the way, Nick," said Bittersohn a bottle or so later, "have you run into Lydia lately?"

Fieringer burped and excused himself too elaborately. "Lydia who?" He was slightly owlish by now.

"Countess Ouspenska. Palmerston's old girlfriend."

"Was she? I never knew that. I don't believe it." Nick's voice was uninterested but he slopped a little of his beer on the nice old Chinese oriental Anora Protheroe had given Sarah during her renovations.

"She says she was," Bittersohn insisted.

"She says she's a countess."

"She calls him Chuckie," Sarah interjected.

"When does she call him Chuckie?" All of a sudden Fieringer was cold sober.

"Last night when they were both visiting here."

The impresario slopped more beer. "What was Lydia doing here?"

"She didn't say. I assumed she merely happened to be in the neighborhood and stopped by to say hello."

"But how could a woman like her know a woman like you?"

Sarah gave him a dose of his own medicine. "Oh, I know everybody. I think the countess is delightful."

"I haven't seen her lately," he answered hollowly. "I haven't seen her for a long time." A few minutes later, Fieringer got up and left.

"Now what the flaming hell," said Bittersohn, "is eating him?"

"He's afraid you don't love him any more."

"I don't think I do. I'm not sure I ever did."

"I've been wondering whether anybody does."

"Oh, sure, Nick has lots of — I see what you mean."

"It's tragic, isn't it? One shouldn't blame him for being what he is."

"I can blame him," Bittersohn replied grimly. "My great old pal, knifing me in the back to keep on the right side of that bastard Palmerston."

"Has it occurred to you that it wasn't on account of Palmerston he wanted the hunt called off?"

"If you really think he's the man behind the robberies, you should have had sense enough not to stay up here alone with him."

"He wouldn't have dared try anything. He knew I'd only to touch the bell and Charles would come rushing up, because I kept ringing for more beer. I knew I had to keep him here till you got back. Believe me, it wasn't a job I'd have taken on for the fun of it."

"Greater love hath no woman." Bittersohn put out a tentative hand toward her, then decided he hadn't better. "Thanks, Sarah, but for God's sake be careful."

"I am, don't worry. Tell me, how did you make out in Brookline?"

"I learned one thing: whoever's doing those copies for the Madam's, it sure as hell isn't Lupe's friend Bengo."

"It wasn't Rembrandt's cat?"

"It wasn't Rembrandt's anything. That jerk must have been stoned to the eyeballs. He got hold of the wrong postcard and copied a Botticelli."

"Was it a good Botticelli?"

"There's no such thing as a good Botticelli." Bittersohn had violent personal opinions about the field he worked in, though he seldom expressed them to his clients.

"Don't be so superior. You know what I mean."

"I suppose with enough dirty varnish and a beat-up gold frame it might fool a blind man in a bad light. At least he saved me from having to buy the picture. I got sore and said it was Rembrandt's cat or nothing, and flounced off in a huff."

"Didn't Lupe promise to have the cat ready for you in a few days?"

"No, he seemed fairly indifferent about the whole deal. I suppose he didn't care because he'd already collected a wad from Palmerston. And an extra commission from my old buddy Nick, no doubt. I wish I knew who actually engineered the Ruy Lopez deal and whether or not Palmerston knew he had a ringer slipped in. Does he have a secretary?"

"I shouldn't be surprised, though I can't say for sure. He does have his odd-job lady Dolores Tawne, and he had Lydia Ouspenska last night."

"How do you know?"

"Don't be salacious. I've had all the bawdry I can take for one evening. Anyway, you know as well as I do that they left here together. And he was surprised and angry to see her here and got her away as fast as he could, and it might have been because he didn't want her to start talking about transatlantic phone calls before he was ready to spring Ruy Lopez on you."

"Why would he get Lydia to make the calls?"

"I don't know. Because he's the sort of person who always orders other people to do things he could perfectly well do for himself, I suppose."

"He'd have to be an awful idiot to entrust any sort of responsibility to Lydia."

"But he is an awful idiot. At least Aunt Caroline and Leila Lackridge always said he was. And look what a fool he made of himself with Mrs. Sorpende at the Madam's yesterday. Maybe he was used to relying on Lydia's opinions about art back in their courting days. She is a really good painter in her way, and perhaps she does know something about art in general. He did say he'd discussed the choosing of an expert with various people whose opinions he values, and she might have been one of them. If he did, couldn't she and Mr. Fieringer have cooked up the Ruy Lopez thing between them? She wouldn't see the implications for you, she'd just think it was a jolly bohemian joke to play on the old goat who jilted her. Maybe that's why Mr. Fieringer denied that she'd been Palmerston's girl friend when he claims to know all about everybody, and why he left in such a hurry after the subject came up."

"You're full of ideas lately aren't you, madam?"

"Why have you started calling me madam all of a sudden?"

"Hell, I can't say Sarah in front of the troops, and surely you don't expect me to say Mrs. Kelling any more. Sarah, did you honestly mean what you told me last night?"

"Yes, Max. All of it."

"Then I guess I'd better go take another cold shower. In case you don't realize it, all this noble high-mindedness is doing one hell of a job on your water bill."

CHAPTER 17

The late breakfasters were sitting around the table the following morning when who should come along, chirpy as a chickadee, but Brooks Kelling. "Thought I'd pay a morning call while I'm out for my constitutional," he explained. "Where's Porter-Smith?"

"Gone to work." Sarah handed him a cup of coffee. "We don't all keep bankers' hours, you know."

"I thought accountants might. Why, thank you, Theonia, those muffins look delicious. I meant to show Porter-Smith a few of the pictures I've taken with my miniature camera under varying conditions. We were discussing photography last night."

"Perhaps you would show the pictures to us," Mrs. Sorpende suggested.

"Delighted." With a conjurer's flourish, he plucked them out of her hair and passed them around.

"What's this?" asked Max Bittersohn, who was seldom at his best so early in the day. "A sack of marbles?"

"You're holding it upside down. That's a nest of turtle eggs."

"But where is the mother turtle?" asked Mrs. Sorpende.

"Off doing her thing somewhere. Turtles are lousy mothers. She just lays 'em and leaves 'em."

"Sounds like Lydia Ouspenska," said Bittersohn.

"And she never gets to see her babies." Mrs. Sorpende was quite properly ignoring such ribaldry. "How sad."

"Here's one baby a mother must have had a hard time loving," Sarah remarked. "Who's this particularly repulsive man? One of our relatives? I'm sure I've met him somewhere."

Cousin Brooks picked up the tiny print and held it far-sightedly at arms length. "Yes, you have. That's Brown, the chapel guard. I particularly wanted Porter-Smith to see this one because I took it with only one overhead sixty-watt bulb for light, down in the locker room."

"Where he drank the paint remover?"

"That's right. Before he drank it, of course. Drat! Sarah, give me those snapshots for a second." Brooks riffled through the stack, pulled one out, and laid it beside the picture of Brown. "Take a gander at this, Bittersohn."

"Well, I'll be damned! Got a glass, Kelling?"

"Certainly." Cousin Brooks whipped a small magnifying glass out of his vest pocket. Together the two men scanned the faces feature by feature.

Sarah craned her neck to see. "Why, that's the one you took of the so-called Dr. Ruy Lopez. Except for his being so much thinner and having that silly beard, you might take him for Brown. What a strange coincidence."

"Coincidence my eyeball," said Bittersohn gallantly. "Kelling, may I keep these?"

"Delighted, my boy. Can I be of further service?"

"Damn right you can. Find out all you can about Brown's background. Check into Fitzroy's alibis. And be careful how you go about it. I don't want anybody spiking your private jug with paint remover."

"Don't keep one. Don't need it. Meet me for lunch at the Burnt Bagel on Longwood Avenue at one o'clock. I'll give you a progress report then. Provided, of course, that I've made any progress. Theonia, don't forget our date."

"How could I? I am looking forward to the lecture on 'The Life of the Angleworm' with eager anticipation."

Brooks buzzed off full of beans. The fair Theonia departed for the tea shop. Bittersohn disappeared who knew where and Sarah helped Mariposa with the breakfast dishes. About half-past two, while Sarah was polishing silver and Mariposa had gone shopping for a new uniform because she was tired of alternating between orange and magenta, Bittersohn came in with a pot of white hyacinths in his hand and a pleased expression on his face.

"For you, madam."

"To feed my soul? How lovely." She gave him the kiss he seemed to think he deserved. "What did you learn about Brown?"

"He had a record. Two years for robbery with assault. It should have been more but his family had influence."

"One wouldn't have thought he came from that sort of family."

"What a snobby little WASP you are. There's influence and influence. Theirs is the other kind."

"You mean they're Godfathers or something? What's their name? Not Brown, surely?"

"No, it's Lupezziz."

"Wasn't that the name of the judge who was indicted for taking bribes some time back?"

"Yes, he's one of the clan. The case was dropped for lack of evidence. It generally is. They're an enterprising family and they stick together, by and large. I guess that's why they made Brown change his name. He blotted the escutcheon by letting himself get busted, though no doubt they kept him as an odd-job man. I wish I knew whether he was on family business at the Madam's, and why Nick just happened to choose Brown's nephew to play the visiting expert."

"How can you find out?"

"Who knows? Maybe I'll go and get myself seduced by Lydia Ouspenska."

"Bring her back to dinner if you're not too tired afterward."

"Funny, aren't you?"

He rumpled the hair Sarah had taken extra pains with that morning and left, walking in his usual fashion, as if he were battling winds of gale force. Sarah combed her hair, finished the silver, did the advance preparation for dinner, then decided it wouldn't hurt her to get out for a breath of air. Thinking she might cross over and walk along the Esplanade for a while, she strolled down to Charles Street.

From force of habit, she looked in at Mr. Hayre's window. The Staffordshire pugs were gone. The new center of interest was an icon, very lovely and very old. Or was it? Sarah pressed her dainty nose against the glass and examined the charming piece until she'd satisfied herself. No doubt about it, here was Lydia Ouspenska's latest artistry. On impulse she opened the door.

"Good afternoon, Mr. Hayre."

"Why, Mrs. Kelling. Long time no see."

"No, I've been too solvent to sell and too poor to buy. I couldn't resist inquiring about that icon in the window, though."

"Now, there," cried Mr. Hayre, "is a find. Did you notice the perfect state of preservation?"

"Yes indeed. It looks as if it had been painted only yesterday," Sarah replied sweetly.

"Doesn't it, though?" The dealer plucked the icon out from among the other pieces and turned it reverently in his pudgy fingers. "It ought to be in a museum, really."

"I'm surprised it isn't. I suppose you're asking a frightful price."

"Well now, to an old friend like you — "

"Hi, Jack." A slim, dark form glided in from the street. "Hi, Mrs. Kelling."

Sarah and Hayre both started. White teeth flashed in Bill Jones's swarthy, delicate face.

"How they going, Bill?" said Hayre with a tinge of uneasiness. "I didn't know you were acquainted with Mrs. Kelling."

"Su-ure. She's got a nice little thing going with Max Bittersohn."

"Mr. Bittersohn is one of my boarders," Sarah explained primly. "Do you know him, Mr. Hayre?"

"I've met him." The antique dealer laid the icon behind the cash register and became ever so busy rearranging his stock.

Sarah took the hint. "Well, since I'm not in the market I mustn't take up your time. Good-bye, Mr. Hayre, Mr. Jones."

But when she reached the door, Bill Jones was at her side. "Can I buy you a drink?" he muttered out of the corner of his mouth.

Sarah had no particular reason to refuse and possibly one to accept. "Why, thank you," she replied. "I'd love one. Though I haven't too much time," she added to be on the safe side. "Could we just go into the lounge here?"

"Su-ure."

A few minutes later they were seated in the darkest booth in the farthest corner of the most obscure cocktail lounge on Charles Street. Bill had got remarkably quick service. Sarah took a taste of her daiquiri and smiled.

"This is a pleasant surprise. How nice of you to ask me, and why do you suppose Mr. Hayre was in such a rush to get rid of me?"

Bill shrugged his shoulders up to his eyebrows, waved his diminutive hands, and leaned over the table. "Jack's a funny guy," he confided.

"He's a businessman at any rate. I sold him some things a few months ago when I was rather frantic for ready cash, and I'd swear he made a thousand per cent profit on every piece."

"Su-ure," breathed the artist. He began drawing pictures in the air with the tip of one exquisite but dirty finger. "It's hard to imagine you being hard up."

"Why do you think I run a boarding house?"

"Why does anybody do anything?"

"Because we can't think of a less disagreeable alternative, I suppose."

"Ah" — Bill leaned even farther over the table, his immense black eyes gleaming through the gloom — "but why can't we?"

"I suppose it depends on our circumstances, early conditioning, personality, one thing and another."

"Yeah-h!"

"It is rather odd, I suppose, that I decided to stick it out in Boston and do this boarding house thing. I could have let the bank have the property, taken whatever cash I could raise, and gone off to Pago Pago or Saskatchewan."

"Or Greece!"

Sarah laughed at his enthusiasm. "Or India."

"I don't think you'd like India. I was there once." He drew some more pictures. "It's not your sort of place."

"What is my sort of place?"

"Oh-h, maybe Paris. I mean, you're" — he did some remarkably effective graphics with both hands. "In a nice way, of course."

"Why, thank you, Bill. May I call you Bill?" Maybe it was the drink, but she was finding this great fun.

"Su-ure," he murmured. "Sarah."

They smiled at each other furtively, as seemed fitting.

"Maxie's a lucky guy," Bill whispered.

"Bill, I've told you — " Sarah stopped. What was the sense in lying to a thoroughly honest man? She changed the subject. "You know Countess Ouspenska, don't you?"

"Doesn't everybody?"

"Max was going to see her this afternoon."

"Hey-y-y." Bill laid a hand over Sarah's. They were about the same size, and Sarah always had trouble finding gloves small enough to fit her. "You're not worried about Maxie and old Lydia?"

"Of course not." Sarah wondered whether she ought to snatch her hand away, but decided Bill's was too small to count. "Unless she takes a notion to seduce him at gunpoint. I do think that's awfully dangerous, don't you? Besides, isn't it against the law now?"

"Seducing Max?"

"No, carrying a handgun."

"What handgun?"

"Her own, I assume. I hope she has a permit for it."

Bill squirmed. "What makes you think Lydia has a gun?"

"I saw it."

"When?"

For Bill Jones, the question was startlingly abrupt. Sarah's pleasant feeling of relaxation vanished. Suppose she told Bill about having gone to Lupe's with Max after they'd trailed Bernie and the countess from Hayre's antique shop? Suppose Bill passed the word back to Hayre and Hayre told Nick Fieringer. Or somebody else. Suppose they change the subject.

"Let's see, when was it? I first met the countess when we met at Dolores Tawne's studio. Then she invited me to her own place. They're neighbors at the Fenway Studios, as you may know. They she dropped in at my house a couple of nights ago. Perhaps I noticed the gun in her handbag when she was fixing her lipstick or something. She carries a great satchel affair. Anyway, I didn't say anything about the gun, of course, and I don't recall that anyone else did, so perhaps it was when we were in the studio. No, thanks, I mustn't have another. I should get home and see how Max made out. Oh dear, that was a slip, wasn't it? I do like her enormously and I'm not the least bit jealous, truly, but she does tend to run on about the magnificent Max. Would you care to walk back with me and join us for sherry?"

"Thanks, but I have a little errand to do," Bill muttered. "I don't suppose you'd be interested in dropping around at my pad later?"

"I don't know what Max's plans are."

"Who said anything about Max?"

Sarah blushed and dimpled. "Oh, I couldn't possibly, but it's sweet of you to ask. Thank you for the drink."

They parted at the door. Sarah turned up Mount Vernon Street. The last she saw of Bill Jones he was headed for Cambridge Street Station, hugging the sides of the buildings.

CHAPTER 18

She was late getting home again, though not so disastrously as she'd been the day she got stuck in her blouse. She let herself in through the alley door and got busy with dinner while Mariposa was doing the drinks in the library. She was chopping and stirring like mad when Bittersohn rushed in, furious with worry.

"Mind telling me where the hell you've been?"

"Having a drink with a charming gentleman."

"I thought something had happened to you."

"Sorry to disappoint you."

He fumed in silence for a moment, then remarked far too casually, "I suppose it was your Uncle Jem."

"No, as a matter of fact it was Bill Jones."

"What were you doing with Bill Jones?"

"I told you, having a drink."

"Why?"

"He invited me."

"So?"

"We met in Mr. Hayre's antique shop."

"Sarah, for Christ's sake what were you doing there?"

"Admiring an authentic early Byzantine icon by Lydia Ouspenska. How did you make out with her, by the way? Or did you?"

"Cut it out, will you? I brought her back to dinner as you told me to. You're some hostess, I must say."

"I'm sure Mrs. Sorpende is coping."

"What did Bill have to say?" Bittersohn demanded after a short pause for silent fuming.

Sarah smiled enigmatically. "A number of things."

"Did he tell you the icon was a fake?"

"Of course not."

"Did you tell him?"

"Why should I bother? I'm sure he knows. I did happen to mention that the countess carries a gun."

"Nice going. Now he knows we followed her to Brookline."

"Not from me he doesn't. I pretended I'd

seen it the night she came here."

Bittersohn grunted. "What did he say when you told him?"

"He was surprised and upset, I think. I have a sneaky hunch he may be on his way to see her right now."

"How can he be? She's here."

"He doesn't know that."

"Why didn't you bring him back with you if you're so fond of his company?"

"I invited him for sherry but he had to go to the countess's. Why are you bothering me about this stuff when I'm running so late already? Did Her Highness dress for dinner?"

"Did she ever!"

"Then go tell her how nice she looks. I'll be right in."

Sarah was used to quick changes by now. About three minutes later she was sweeping into the library. "Countess Ouspenska, do forgive me for not being here to welcome you. We're so glad you could come."

"Me too!" screamed Lydia, flashing a smile at Mr. Porter-Smith. She certainly had dressed. Her gown was of scarlet crepe circa 1935, cut low in the front and lower in the back. A huge purple silk anemone rode on her left hipbone. She had bracelets up to the elbows and earrings down to her collarbones.

234

In her raddled way she was gorgeous.

When Charles announced dinner she swept grandly in on the arm of Porter-Smith, to whom she had taken an obvious fancy. That dapper young blade had blossomed out in a new Madras dinner jacket of a lightsome yellow and green plaid. Together he and the countess were resplendent to the point of dazzlement. Even Professor Ormsby's eyes were seen to stray for a moment from Mrs. Sorpende's impressive façade, but the countess was too skinny for his taste so they soon strayed back.

Lydia Ouspenska was in the liveliest possible spirits. She laughed uproariously at everyone's jokes, especially her own. She took lavish helpings of everything Charles passed. Then suddenly she clapped a hand to her mouth and staggered to her feet.

Charles had her out of the dining room almost before the others realized what was happening. Sarah rose to follow but Porter-Smith beat her to it. "Allow me, Mrs. Kelling. I have my Senior Lifesaving Badge."

Knowing her efficient staff would cope, Sarah tried to carry on as a good hostess should. Charles was back in time to serve dessert. He reported that the countess appeared to be resting more comfortably and Mariposa was with her. As the group moved back to the library for coffee, though, Sarah thought she'd better scoot up for a peek herself.

Charles, Mariposa, and no doubt the unflappable Mr. Porter-Smith himself had got the poor countess to bed most efficiently. Somebody had even remembered to turn back the counterpane and lay a clean sheet over the blanket cover before bundling her up in the eiderdown. The flamboyant red gown was folded neatly over the back of Sarah's low slipper chair, the bangles stacked on the night stand, the gold sandals set side by side on the rug. Lydia was not only asleep but snoring loudly.

Remembering the woman's hit-or-miss eating habits, Sarah decided a gastric upset was most likely due to the shock of her system's trying to ingest a square meal for a change. She closed the door and went downstairs to drink her coffee with an easier mind.

Her boarders were all being terribly understanding about the incident. Mrs. Sorpende was spinning a pathetic picture of the infant countess fleeing the Winter Palace with wolves and Bolsheviki in rabid pursuit, growing up as a fragile waif on the streets of Istanbul or some such exotic place, peddling her jewel-encrusted Easter eggs to buy croissants and brioches. It was a gripping story and Sarah thought it was too bad the countess couldn't be there to hear. Still she was relieved when it came to an end and she could go back to check on the patient. She wasn't at all surprised when Max Bittersohn came, too.

By now Lydia seemed even deeper in slumber, her breath coming in gasps and gurgles. "Out like a light," said Max. "She must have loaded up on that wine you sent her while I was waiting downstairs for her to get dressed."

"What wine?" Sarah asked him. "I only sent food."

"That's funny. There was a bottle sitting on the table by her stairway. I took it for granted — " He bent over the sleeping woman, beginning to look anxious.

Sarah ducked under his elbow. "She's making awfully strange noises. I can't see her color under all that goop on her face. Bring me the jar of cold cream from the bathroom shelf, will you? And a towel."

She was feeling for a pulse when Bittersohn dashed back with the cold cream and her very best lace-trimmed guest towel. "Here" — Sarah handed the limp wrist over to him — "you try. I never have any luck with pulses." She smeared cold cream on the painted cheeks and began to wipe. The bared skin was oddly bluish in color. "Max, this doesn't look awfully good to me."

He scowled. "The pulse is so light I can hardly feel it. Ring for Charlie. Tell him to get a cab quick."

"Do you think there may have been some kind of slow-acting poison in that wine?"

"I don't know, but after what happened to Brown we'd better not take any chances."

They bundled the unconscious woman up in blankets and rushed her to the emergency entrance of the hospital. The intern on duty looked at Lydia's color, listened to her heart, scratched his head, and sent for a resident. The resident probed, rolled up an eyelid, peered, and sent for a laboratory technician. Sarah and Max were bombarded with questions. Where had she been? What had she eaten? What was her medical history? Who was her next of kin?

At the last question Sarah burst into tears. "Can't you tell us what's the matter with her?" she sobbed.

"Maybe it's an allergic reaction," ventured the intern.

"Maybe we'd better get a stomach pump and an oxygen mask," said the resident.

They wheeled Countess Ouspenska away, leaving Sarah and Max to answer as best they could the questions of a weary admitting clerk. When they'd managed that, Sarah said, "We'd better wait."

"It might be a while," he reminded her.

"I don't care. I feel responsible. What if it was something I cooked?"

"Then you and I would be sick, too, wouldn't we?"

"But an allergy — "

"Allergy hell!"

The seats in the waiting room became desperately uncomfortable. Bittersohn prowled back and forth along the corridors, bringing back things out of vending machines he found: coffee that tasted like nothing in particular, stale crackers filled with what was supposed to be peanut butter and tasted like shellac, candy bars loaded with sugar and sickish artificial flavorings. Sarah didn't even attempt to eat them. After a while she found a pay phone and called the house.

"Charles, is everybody else all right? Then it can't possibly have been food poisoning.

239

No, they haven't told us a thing. Yes, as far as I know she's still — I'm sure they're doing everything they can. Don't wait up. I have my key and Mr. Bittersohn is staying with me."

She rang off and went back to join him. "Everything's fine back there. What I can't understand is why it should have taken so long to work, if it was poison. She was in the house for almost two hours before she got so horribly sick all of a sudden. She didn't offer you any of that wine, I hope?"

"No. She did say something about making a glass of tea but I told her not to bother."

"How long were you in the studio?"

"Maybe an hour."

"What were you doing?"

"Talking. Listening, I should say. You know Lydia."

"What was she talking about?"

"Life, love, the problems of the creative artist, who knows? Lydia was in a peculiar mood. I'd lead her up to a subject and she'd turn kittenish on me. She says she hasn't seen Nick Fieringer in years, which I suspect is a lie. She claims Palmerston's still crazy about her, which I know damn well must be a lie. All I got out of her is that the man in her bed that night was Bill

Jones, and that doesn't mean a thing."

"Why doesn't it?"

"Because Bill sleeps there half the time, or so she claims. His buddies are always wanting to use his pad for one reason or another. If he gets sleepy and it's too late to bother any of his girl friends, he pops over and crawls in with Lydia. 'Is purely Plutonic," she says."

"I'll bet it is! Max, shouldn't we go over to her studio and collar that bottle of wine before somebody else does?"

"If it's poisoned and traceable, somebody already has, no doubt. If it isn't, why bother? Furthermore, my adorable little fuzzyhead, that's what's known as tampering with evidence."

"Oh."

They sat awhile longer, then Sarah asked, "Did Brooks find out anything about Mr. Fitzroy?"

"Yes. On Sunday when Witherspoon was killed, Fitzroy was attending a family reunion in Topsfield with about eighty-seven other Fitzroys. On Monday when Brown was killed, Fitzroy was with one or the other of the guards every damned minute of the time, mainly giving them all hell for letting things get out of hand while he was away. Brooks is inclined to think he's a washout and so am I. His bank balance and style of living are consistent with his position, and his character is so irreproachable it's pitiful."

"I'm so sorry, darling." Sarah patted Max's hand and went to find a ladies' room. She spent quite a while doing things to her face and hair, then got in a panic for fear she might have missed a report from the doctor and ran out with one lock streaming loose.

"Why don't you go fix your hair?" said Bittersohn.

She went back and fixed it. They sat some more. Then Sarah asked, "Where had she been before you got there?"

Bittersohn jerked upright. "Where what?"

"I'm sorry, I didn't realize you were asleep."

"I wasn't asleep," he said huffily, "I was thinking."

"About what?"

"Mmh?"

Sarah picked up a newspaper somebody had discarded and read about bodies found in lonely lanes. Bittersohn's head fell heavily but agreeably against her shoulder. She eased it to a more comfortable position, rested her cheek against the luxuriant dark brown waves of his hair, and did the crossword puzzle. She had turned to the sports section and was wondering how one went about handicapping a horse when the intern came out.

"It was a mixture of arsenic and Nembutal," he told her. "Dr. Fingerford says you're to wait till the police get here."

CHAPTER 19

Between them, Sarah and Max knew just about every policeman on the Boston force by now. When uniformed officers Moynahan and Maloney showed up in the cruiser they merely remarked, "Oh, Jesus, you two again," and sent for plainclothes detectives Fitzpatrick and Fitzgibbon. The latter pair, when they arrived, said much the same thing.

"Okay, Mrs. Kelling," Fitzgibbon began, "mind telling us how you happened to be entertaining this alleged Countess Ouspenska?"

"I met her just this past week through Mrs. Tawne, an artist who's a friend of my cousin Brooks Kelling. The countess and Mrs. Tawne are neighbors in the Fenway Studios on Ipswich Street. Mrs. Tawne had me over to tea. While I was there, the countess dropped in and invited me to see her studio. Then the other night she dropped by the house. My boarders thought she was fun, so I asked Mr. Bittersohn to bring her back to dinner this evening."

"Old friend of yours, Bittersohn?" asked Fitzpatrick.

"If you mean what I think you do, no. I have known her for some years on a casual basis. I mentioned to Mrs. Kelling this afternoon that I was going to see Lydia, and she asked me to pass on the invitation. It was a spur-of-the-moment thing."

"That's right," Sarah confirmed. "I didn't know whether or not she'd come until she arrived."

"What did you give her to eat?"

"Only what the rest of us had." Sarah recited the menu. "I didn't get into the library, where we usually gather before dinner, until shortly after she'd arrived but I'm told she was shown directly there. Some of my other boarders were already present. She had sherry out of the same decanter as everybody else and hors d'oeuvres from the same tray. When we went in to dinner she helped herself from the same dishes that were passed to us all. The countess seemed to be in excellent spirits and ate a great deal. I knew she had very irregular eating habits, so when she got sick to her stomach, I simply assumed she'd eaten too much too fast."

"Um. Bittersohn, you were with this Ouspenska woman for how long before the dinner party? Did you come back to Mrs. Kelling's together, or what?"

"We drove back together in my car. Before that, I was in her studio for perhaps an hour."

"Doing what?"

"Talking. She happens to be an expert on Byzantine icons."

"Whatever they are. Did you have a drink with her or anything?"

"No. I saw a bottle of wine on the table, but she didn't offer me any. She may have eaten or drunk something while she was in the back room changing her clothes."

"Or taken a pill," Sarah put in.

"Why a pill?" said Fitzgibbon.

"Oh, I don't know. It just occurred to me, I suppose because she's not a young woman. I have a lot of middle-aged aunts and they all take pills for one thing or another. Don't yours?"

"Jeez, yes, come to think of it. My Aunt Theresa, every time she comes over to the house she lines up about six different pill bottles in front of her and pops 'em down one after the other like they were candy."

Max and his Aunt Fruma did the same

thing, and Fitzpatrick was trying to get in a word about his Aunt Mary Margaret when Fitzgibbon intervened.

"Who'd know about the pills? This neighbor of hers you mentioned, they're pretty good friends, eh?"

"I don't know whether you'd call them friends or not. Mrs. Tawne told me the countess had a habit of dropping in at mealtimes, so I daresay she might have mentioned her health problems on some such occasion, if she has any. The countess isn't what you'd call the reticent type."

"Maybe we'd better go and find out."

"At this hour?" Tears of exhaustion stung Sarah's eyelids. "Mrs. Tawne's not a young woman either, and she must have been in bed ages ago."

"Too bad," said Fitzgibbon, "but it looks to me like we have a case of attempted murder on our hands, and maybe Mrs. Tawne got tired of being mooched on. If she was feeding the Ouspenska woman all the time, she'd have a pretty good chance of slipping something into the food, wouldn't she?"

"I suppose so." Sarah heaved a mighty sigh and followed the two detectives out to their car, grateful for Max Bittersohn's arm to lean on.

As she'd expected, Dolores Tawne was none too happy at being aroused. She came up to her studio door in a pink plissé kimono and a headful of metal curlers such as Sarah had thought nobody in the world except Cousin Mabel still used.

"I'm so sorry," Sarah began in a faltering tone.

"Well, I should think you would be, rioting around with a gang of men at this hour! Brooks gave me to understand you were a respectable woman." She rattled her curlers fiercely at Max.

Fitzgibbon was tired, too. "Are you Mrs. Dolores Tawne?" he snapped.

"I certainly am, and would you kindly tell me what you mean by – ?"

"We're police officers." He stuck his identification and badge under her nose. "Would you mind telling us when you last saw your neighbor Mrs. Ouspenska?"

"I assume you're referring to the woman who calls herself a countess and as far as I know she's still a Miss. I doubt if she's ever bothered to marry any of them. What do you want to know for?"

"For good and sufficient reason, Mrs. Tawne. Would you mind answering the question?"

"Humph! Then I suppose I — let me see, she usually barges in when I'm having my cup of tea around four o'clock. Was it then? No, I was at the museum this afternoon. Yesterday afternoon I suppose it would be by now. Then we must have bumped into each other earlier in the — er — facilities. Neither of us has a private bathroom, more's the pity."

"How did she seem to you? Was she in her usual spirits?" asked Fitzpatrick.

"She was feeling the effects of her usual spirits if that's what you mean. Any woman her age who goes out every night till all hours and drinks with riffraff has only herself to blame, as I've told her time and again."

"In other words she had a hangover?"

"You could call it that."

"Would you say she was seriously depressed?"

"She's always depressed, always whining and wailing about getting old and losing her looks. A decent woman shouldn't have to worry about anything except being clean and covered." Dolores hitched the shapeless kimono more closely around her barrel-like form.

"Has she ever mentioned suicide in your hearing?"

"Not more than once every five minutes. Downright wickedness I call it, making jokes about a thing like that."

"What sorts of jokes?"

"Oh, Russian roulette. She was claiming the other day she's invented a new version. She's going to fill one of her stomach capsules with poison and — look here, I have a right to know why you're asking me this stuff."

Fitzgibbon told her. "Because Countess Ouspenska is in the hospital with arsenic poisoning and we'd like to know how she got it."

"Oh, my God! Then I'm responsible."

"Why?"

"Because" — Dolores rubbed her square, red palm across her square, red face — "I didn't think she meant it. I thought it was just more of her foolishness. I should have stopped it."

"How could you?"

"I don't know. Taken away the capsules, maybe." Dolores collapsed into a chair. "I just don't know."

"Now, take it easy, Mrs. Tawne," said Fitzpatrick, who was a kind man. "You can't blame yourself if somebody decides to pull a half-wit stunt like that. Do you remember exactly what she told you?"

"As nearly as I can recall, she said she was going to take the medicine out of one of her digestive capsules — she has awful stomach trouble on account of the way she eats, or doesn't eat. Well, anyway, she said she'd fill the capsule with poison and mix it in with the rest. That way she'd never know when she was taking the poison. It would be more fun to be surprised. That's what she said, more fun. I told her to stop acting so silly and she laughed at me." Dolores began to cry.

Sarah slipped an arm around the beefy shoulders. "Now, Mrs. Tawne, please don't take it to heart so. She may still come out of it all right. The doctors are doing all they can. Why don't you make yourself a nice cup of tea and go back to bed?"

"Sure," said Fitzgibbon, "we'll clear out and let you sleep. Is there any way we can get into Countess Ouspenska's studio, do you know?"

"Just open the door, most likely. She forgets to lock up more often than not. It's the second door from this one on the right."

As Dolores had predicted, the door was unlocked. They filed in. Bittersohn found a light switch and achieved a feeble glow from a twenty-watt amber bulb.

"Jeez," said Fitzgibbon, "this place looks like a rummage sale. She must be some kind of a nut all right."

"She's an artist," said Sarah. For some reason she felt duty-bound to stick up for the countess.

"Yeah? Where would she keep the pills, I wonder?"

"They could be anywhere." Sarah looked around at the maze of furniture and bric-a-brac. "I should think by her bed or over the sink. There's a little back room and a sort of kitchenette through here at the back."

The group picked their way through the confusion and found the bed. In calm repose on its grimy pillows lay the curly head of Bill Jones.

"Bill," shouted Fitzpatrick, "what are you doing here?"

The artist flung off the covers and sat up. He was attired only in a pair of lavender satin shorts. "Oh, hi, Fitz. Hi, Sarah. Hi, Max. What gives?"

"You a friend of this Ouspenska woman, Bill?" In view of the lavender shorts, Fitzpatrick's question seemed redundant.

"Su-ure. Lydia's an old pal of mine. Some of the boys wanted to use the pad tonight

252

and I wasn't going to be needing it myself," he added with the barest flicker of a glance at Sarah, "so I sacked out here. Hey, how come the delegation? Is Lydia okay?"

"She's down at the Mass. General with a bellyful of arsenic."

"No-o-o!"

"Has she ever said anything to you about playing Russian roulette with her stomach pills?"

"Su-ure, but hey, you mean she wasn't putting me on?"

"That remains to be seen. Can you think of any way she might have got hold of some arsenic?"

"Pal, the cats she hangs out with could get hold of a hydrogen bomb."

"Yeah? Well, I guess that more or less ties it. Cover up, Bill, you'll catch cold. Just for the record, you don't happen to know where she keeps the pills, do you?"

"Right over there."

A bottle of immense yellow and green capsules was sitting in plain sight on the dresser. Fitzpatrick wrapped it carefully in a tissue and put it in a little box he took from his pocket. "Easy enough to take one of these things apart and reload it. The gelatin would take a little while to dissolve, especially on a full stomach, so she wouldn't feel the effects right away. Arsenic doesn't act all that fast anyway. That heavy meal she ate probably saved her life. Chances are it did upset her stomach so that she got rid of some of the poison before it had a chance to work. I suppose her idea was that the Nembutal would knock her out so she wouldn't feel the pain when the arsenic began to work. We'll have the lab check the rest of these out, just to give them something to do."

"Say," said Fitzgibbon, "how about if this guy here loaded those knockout drops himself? Maybe it's a crime of passion or something."

"Are you kidding? This is Pericles Jonubopoulos's baby brother."

"Oh. Hey, pal, no offense?"

"Forget it, pal," said Bill magnanimously. "Hey, no kidding, is Lydia going to be okay? Should I go over to the hospital?"

"They wouldn't let you see her," Bittersohn told him. "Sarah and I couldn't get into the room, either. She's pretty sick, because she was in rough shape to start with, but the doctor thinks she has a fighting chance."

"Then I might as well grab a little more sacktime. Night, Sarah. Night, Max. Night, Fitz. Night, pal." The baby brother of

Pericles Jonubopoulos smiled sweetly at them all, pulled the once white sheet up over his slim brown torso, and went back to sleep.

Sarah kept her lips buttoned until the two Fitzes had dropped her and Bittersohn off at Tulip Street. Then she exploded.

"How damnably convenient!"

"Isn't it, though. I think I'll go back and have another little chat with Bill."

"Max, it's so late."

"I only hope it's not too late. Damn it, Sarah, I'm scared."

"Then let's go and get it over with."

"Maybe you'd rather I sent you alone. You could use your feminine wiles." He slipped his arms around her and leaned his head on hers. "How come Bill calls you Sarah?"

"Think nothing of it. He knows I have a nice little thing going with Max Bittersohn. He said so to Mr. Hayre. Anyway, I haven't a wile left in me. You don't honestly believe Bill tried to murder Lydia Ouspenska?"

"How could I? He's Pericles Jonubopoulos's baby brother. I think Bill knows something. Bill likes knowing things. You'd better go in the house and get some sleep."

"No, please, I want to stay with you. It's too awful, people popping off all over the place and the police just saying tough luck and going away."

"You can't blame the police too much. They don't know a possible connection exists between Lydia and the two guards at the Wilkins."

"And you didn't tell them because you want to do it all yourself."

"I don't particularly want to, but I have to now that Palmerston's boxed me in. You know that. Let's see if we can pick up a cab on Beacon, if you can walk that far."

"I'm so tired it doesn't matter any more. Come on." They walked a moment in silence, then Sarah remarked, "You know, whoever is doing these things must be awfully well informed. He'd have had to know about Witherspoon's dizzy spells and Brown's hidden bottle and Lydia's new joke about her stomach pills, which I suppose doesn't mean a thing, because Brown was Lupe's uncle and Lupe is Bernie's pal and Bernie is Lydia's and Lydia is Dolores's neighbor and everybody seems to be connected with everybody one way or another. Bernie could have put that stuff in Lydia's capsule while they were together, couldn't he?"

"Why not?"

"If he did, Mr. Fieringer put him up to it, right?"

"You might ask Nick," said Bittersohn. "There he goes now."

The hulking figure of the impresario was moving away from the studio building as they approached. They could see his yellow face clearly enough in the light over the steps. For once Nick wasn't smiling. He paid no attention to them but turned the corner and walked up past the Catholic church.

"Going home, I expect," said Bittersohn. "He has an apartment over on Hemenway Street. Come on."

They went up to the third floor, tiptoed along the creaky wooden corridor that reeked pleasantly of linseed oil and turpentine, and pushed open the door of Lydia Ouspenska's studio. Through the dark came Bill Jones's sleepy voice.

"What's the matter, Nick? Forget something?"

CHAPTER 20

"Nick went along," said Bittersohn. "It's Sarah and Max. Mind if we come down for a second?"

"No-o." There was the barest shade of irritation in the soft voice as Bill got up and switched on the lights so they wouldn't break their necks on the stairs from the balcony. "I might as well have stayed for the game. There's more action here tonight than in my own pad."

"Sorry, Bill. That'll teach you to sack in with Plutonic women. How long did Nick stay?"

"Long enough to say good-bye. He was looking for Lydia."

"Did you tell him about the Russian roulette?"

"Su-ure. Why not?"

"What does he think?"

Bill began to draw pictures in the air. "Nick says it just goes to show. Nobody ever knows anybody."

"In other words he doesn't believe it, either."

"What can I say, Maxie? Everybody figured she was putting us on. You know Lydia. I mean as well as anybody can know anybody."

"No, I don't know her that well, but I know her. Damn it, Lydia was having a ball tonight. Wasn't she, Sarah?"

"She certainly was and nobody can tell me for one moment that she ever thought seriously of suicide. And if she ever did, she wouldn't pick anything quiet and messy and painful like arsenic. She'd get out in the middle of Boston Common and commit hara-kiri with the sword of Ivan the Terrible or something. And she'd wait till she'd collected a good, big audience around to stop her."

"Yeah-h," said Bill.

"Mind if we take a look around?" Bittersohn asked.

"Why should I? It's not my pad. Oh, hey, maybe I should put on some pants or something?"

"Why don't you just go back to bed?" Sarah suggested.

"No-o. I want to see Maxie detect something. How do you know when you find a clue, pal?"

"I crack my shins on it." Bittersohn was holding up an unfinished canvas and trying to rub paint off his London-tailored trousers with a beautiful Irish linen handkerchief. "What do you think of this?"

Bill, in his lavender shorts and his tiny bare feet, picked his way around, over, and through a welter of stools, taborets, and umbrella stands to get a close look at the canvas. He scratched his jetty curls. "Looks to me like about two thirds of a Murillo."

"That's what it is, pal. There's one just like it at the Madam's. About the only original left, or was as of Sunday as far as I could see. And apparently that one's also slated for removal."

"Yeah-h, but a Murillo? Who's going to buy a hot Murillo?"

"There's always a mark somewhere. Would you say this might be Lydia's work?"

Bill squinted professionally at the canvas. "Lydia's good, you know. Those icons of hers — you've rumbled the icons, of course?"

"Sarah did."

"How about that? Like I was saying, those icons are real works of art. I mean, anybody buys one of those is getting something for his money even if it doesn't happen to be what he thinks he's getting. But this — "

Bill snatched a tasseled silk shade off a dinky boudoir lamp and held the light closer to the painting. "Maxie, can you dig this? I mean, like this isn't a bad job." His free hand made darting motions at the canvas. "Slick. But Lydia's an icon painter. You dig, Maxie?"

Even Sarah dug. Those rigidly stylized miniatures with their meticulous detailing were too different from this voluptuous, swirling candy-box prettiness. One would think some of the formality of the Byzantine technique must be reflected in whatever Lydia did.

"You thought the copies at the Wilkins were all done by the same hand," Bittersohn prompted. "Would this be the one?"

Bill wiggled and squirmed and drew more pictures in the air, to the peril of his slippery satin undergarment. "That's what bugs me. See, Maxie, if Lydia painted all those copies, that means she's kept her mouth shut about them for over thirty years. I mean, can you see Lydia keeping a secret for over thirty minutes? She makes this big cloak-and-dagger deal about Jack Hayre, but how long did it take Sarah to find out?"

"I knew she was faking icons roughly half an hour after I'd met her for the first time and I knew Mr. Hayre was fencing them, or whatever you call it, as soon as I saw that one in his window yesterday," Sarah replied. "I didn't pry, either. Lydia showed me. She was proud of what she was doing. Well she might be, as far as workmanship is concerned. As to the icon, there it was. I couldn't miss, could I?"

"No-o-o."

"So this isn't a painting, it's a frame," said Bittersohn.

"Not bad, Maxie. That could be one answer."

"Care to give me another?"

Bill shrugged and cast a longing glance toward the frowzy bed.

"All right, Bill, go get some rest. We'll let ourselves out quietly when we're through."

Less than a minute later the baby brother of Pericles Jonubopoulos was fast asleep. Sarah and Max continued to rummage.

"Max, look!" Sarah hissed.

Nestled in Lydia's top dresser drawer amid a tangle of wrinkled scarves, ruined panty hose, and odd gloves lay a small plastic phial with a warning label on the side. It had been full of a white powder. Now a quarter inch of the powder was gone.

Bittersohn picked the phial up gingerly

inside a gaudy nylon kerchief and stuck it in his pocket. "I'll give this to Fitz and Fitz. Ten to nothing it's arsenic, and there won't be any fingerprints."

"Sh-h. Don't wake him again."

Bittersohn looked down at the peacefully slumbering Bill, rubbing his own chin, on which stubble was beginning to appear. "You're like the rest of them. Every woman who meets Bill wants to mother him, and the next thing she knows — "

"I know, thank you. I shouldn't dream of wanting to mother him. He's like one of those little cock sparrows you see around the streets, isn't he? Cute and tough and no doubt an egg in every nest. Can you tell me why we didn't spot that Murillo when we were here with the two detectives?"

"Because it wasn't here, naturally."

"That's what Nick Fieringer had been doing when we saw him leaving the building, wasn't it? Do you suppose Mrs. Tawne phoned and told him about the countess? Or could he have learned some other way? Maybe Mr. Hayre had a spy outside the house and saw us take her to — no, that's pretty silly, isn't it? Most likely he came here to plant the arsenic and Bill told him she was already in the hospital and

263

he rushed off to wherever the copies are being done and got the painting, thinking to make her the scapegoat because she was probably going to die anyway."

"Possibly. Let's go ask him."

"You mean wake him up and say, 'Sorry to bother you, but do you happen to be a murderer?'"

"Why not? It's just up around the corner."

Fieringer lived in one of those grim apartment houses whose unclean foyers are floored with chipped tiles in fancy patterns and shut in by heavily varnished doors that are supposed to be kept locked but often are not. Inside was the usual scary little elevator that smelled of urine. People had scrawled initials and indecent suggestions on its walls with magic markers and the sharp ends of door keys. Bittersohn pushed the button for the fourth floor. The cage wobbled upward.

"Shouldn't we have rung his doorbell at least?" Sarah whispered.

"I thought we might as well try shock tactics."

Nick's door, unlike Lydia's, was locked. Bittersohn pounded on the panels. After a longish time they heard the shuffle of slippered feet and a sleepy voice calling out, "Who is it?"

"It's me. Open up." Bittersohn's voice was a fair imitation of Bernie the pianist's.

There was a rattling of chains and bolts, then the door opened. In his pajamas Nick Fieringer was unspeakable. The rumpled pants sagged below his great bare belly, the unbuttoned coat revealed a sparsely haired chest with breasts that sagged like an old woman's. His longish hair stuck up in greasy spikes around the bald spot on top. His yellow face was sunken, his jowls drooped. For a moment he stared at them. Then he pasted a tight-lipped grin on his face and ran a hand over his hair to slick it down.

"Excuse please," he mumbled. He partially closed the door and returned a couple of minutes later decently covered by a bathrobe, his hair carefully combed over his bald spot and his toothy grin in full radiance.

"He's put in his dentures," Sarah thought. She wished she didn't find the man so pathetically disgusting.

The airless one-room apartment was neat enough except for the rumpled studio couch on which Fieringer must have been sleeping. What made it feel so unbearably cluttered were the pictures. Everywhere: thumbtacked to the walls, crowded on the table, the bureau, the imitation marble mantelpiece with no fireplace under it were photographs of the well-known, the lesser-known, the unknown. Many of them were inscribed: To Nick with love, To Nick with Best Wishes, To Nick, To My Good Friend Nick, To Nick from some unfamiliar name scribbled too large. In a few the impresario himself appeared smiling his jack-o'-lantern smile with his arm around some cringing shoulder or his paw clutching some reluctantly extended hand. It was true. He did know everybody.

Bittersohn wasted no time on amenities. "I suppose you know Lydia's been poisoned."

"Lydia who?"

"Knock it off, Nick. Third from the left on the mantelpiece."

Sure enough, there was a photo of the two taken in some nightclub years ago. "To my darling Nickie" was scrawled across the cardboard mount in red crayon. Fieringer waddled over and took a long look at it. Then he turned around.

"Yes, I know."

"Who did it?"

"She did, playing crazy games with her stomach pills."

"Do you believe that?"

The fat man swallowed twice and hitched the cord of his bathrobe tighter around his pendulous abdomen. "I have to, don't I?"

"No."

"Maxie, you don't understand."

"I think I do."

"Then why do you come bothering me now? Why not let an old man get a little sleep?"

"What were you doing at the Fenway Studios about half an hour ago?"

"Looking for Bernie. He plays in concert tomorrow, I want him sober. Sometimes he stays with Lydia. Tonight I find only Bill Jones. Ask Bill."

"What did you take with you?"

"Take? What should I take with me? What's to take?"

"Where did you go before you wound up at Lydia's?"

"Everywhere. Is no job for an old man."

Bittersohn didn't respond to Nick's nervous smile. "Did you see Lupe?"

"Lupe who?"

"Didn't he give you anything?"

"Lupe give? Believe me, my friend, Lupe only takes."

"What were you wearing this evening?"

"Wearing?" This one really puzzled Nick.

"Naturally my suit. On the chair." A pair of gray trousers lay neatly folded across the chair seat, the matching coat hung over the back. "In the morning I press before putting on," he apologized to Sarah.

Bittersohn picked up the clothes and went over them inch by inch. Sarah tried not to watch. The immense trousers with their baggy seat and the wrinkles radiating from the crotch, the cheap jacket with perspiration stains under the armpits were too obscene. This was the same suit he'd worn when he sat sweating and swilling beer in her private sitting room. It was, come to think of it, the only one she'd ever seen on him and likely the only one he owned. What on earth was he doing with all the money he must be getting?

"Where's the shirt you had on?" asked Bittersohn.

"Hanging in the bathroom. I wash every night. Drip-dry, is very convenient," he explained again to Sarah.

She was mortally ashamed to be there. This gross creature trying to keep up appearances, trying to convince himself the whole world loved him, trying to catch a few hours' sleep after a night no man his age should be putting in for any reason good or evil was enough to tear one's heart out. She suspected Max Bittersohn was feeling what she was, but he kept doggedly on, inspecting the damp shirt, the crumpled underwear, finally the man's fat hands. At last, thank God, he was satisfied.

"Okay, Nick."

"Thank you, my friend," said the impresario with about the same degree of gaiety Rigoletto had to display before the jeering courtiers after they had kidnapped his daughter. "Even if I don't know what's okay I'm glad it's okay."

"When you were in Lydia's studio tonight, did you notice an unfinished painting?"

"In a studio is always an unfinished painting. Should I notice?"

"This one was on the floor near the stairs, propped against a little table."

"In Lydia's studio is wall-to-wall little tables. No, my friend, I did not notice."

"Nick, you'd better tell me what you know."

"What should I know?"

"Shove it, Nick. Two guards from the Madam's have already been murdered. Lydia will have been, too, if she doesn't pull through. You know damn well she'd never feed herself anything more poisonous than cheap booze and lousy food. Somebody's trying to frame her as the artist who faked about ninety-seven per cent of the paintings at the Wilkins Museum and sold the originals out of state. I think it could be you."

"Me?" Fieringer's yellow face turned to dirty ivory.

"You were in the right places at the right times. You know the museum setup and routine. You knew Witherspoon and Brown. You're an old boyfriend of Lydia's."

"Who isn't?" shouted the impresario. "Max, I swear to you on the sacred memory of my mother I had nothing to do with stealing the paintings, I had nothing to do with the murders. With Lydia yes. I help her to sell her pretty icons. Is it so terrible to keep an old friend from starving to death?"

"Where do you help her sell them?"

"I fixed up a connection with Jack Hayre on Charles Street." The sweat was pouring down over Nick's flabby jowls. "Only this and nothing more I do. She is the only beautiful woman who would ever go to bed with me."

"Did C. Edwald Palmerston go to bed with you, too? You fixed up that Ruy Lopez deal for him."

270

"Max, what could I do? Palmerston comes pussyfooting to me and starts beating around the bushes. At last it comes out he wants the thefts hushed up to save his face. He doesn't want Palmerston the great philanthropist to become Palmerston the stupid jackass who lets a museum be stolen from under his nose. It is not brave, it is not noble, it is not gentlemanly, but" – he shrugged – "it is human. Palmerston wants a phony expert to make Bittersohn look like the fool, not him. A Jew who didn't even go to Harvard, to him you are expendable. So I think of Lupe because" – he shrugged again – "for a crooked deal I think of Lupe."

"I see. I'm expendable to you as well as to Palmerston."

"Max, I am also expendable. I kid other people a little, maybe. Myself I don't kid. Am I Sol Hurok? Am I Boris Goldovsky? I am old Nick the odd-job man who gets thrown a little something here, a little something there. Who are my great artists? A lush like Bernie, a mediocre student with parents who have money to start her off on a great career you should live so long. I hold the job at the Wilkins all these years because Palmerston is a cheapskate and old Nick is willing to work cheap. I don't go along with what he wants, I lose the concerts. I have nowhere to show off my performers. I am nothing."

He slumped down on top of the wrinkled trousers, his hands dangling loose between his knees.

"Nick," said Bittersohn quietly, "I asked you to tell me what you know."

"Max, I make it my business not to know. For years I think maybe is something funny going on and I shut my eyes. In school back in the old country my teacher used to show three idiot monkeys. Hear no evil, see no evil, speak no evil. Hah! What a thing to tell us then. Before we know two and two we know to steal, to lie, to betray is to stay alive. I lie, sure. But about this I don't lie to you, my friend. I know nothing because I choose to know nothing."

"Then what do you suspect?"

"Suspect?" Fieringer rolled the word around on his tongue as though it were a new sound to him. "I suspect somebody has made from the Madam for a long time a fat living. Do I look like it's me?"

"You could have given the money away," whispered Sarah. "To your friends."

"I could. I have given much. In the end I am still ugly old fat Nick. I stopped giving.

If I could find a way I would take, but I never find a way. Max, I cannot help you. I know nothing. I suspect nobody. I am an old man. I have to sleep. Let me alone." His voice broke. "Please."

Bittersohn turned away. "Come on, Sarah," he sighed, "let's go home."

CHAPTER 21

Sarah checked with the hospital about six times the following day. At five in the evening, while she was making biscuits for dinner, she phoned from the kitchen. Lydia Ouspenska had not yet regained consciousness but she was still alive. The floor nurse sounded surprised.

She'd just got the phone hung up and her hands back in the biscuit dough when Brooks called. "Sarah," he hissed, "tell your young man there's dirty work afoot at the Madam's. I'm going to lurk here and see what's up."

"Brooks," she gasped, "you can't do that!"

"Of course I can. I intend to disguise myself as a fifteenth-century gargoyle."

"You don't know what dreadful risks you may be taking."

"Sensible men don't take risks."

"Sensible men don't disguise themselves as fifteenth-century gargoyles."

"Sarah, I have no time to argue. Would you kindly explain to Theonia that I shan't be able to take her to the Museum of Science tonight."

"You can't trifle with the affections of an honest woman like that."

"Theonia will understand."

"That's what you think. Just a minute, I see Mr. Bittersohn coming in through the alley gate." She thumped on the window, beckoned him up, and thrust the phone at him. "Here, for heaven's sake talk him out of it."

"Him whom?"

"Cousin Brooks. He says something's going on at the Madam's and he's going to disguise himself as a fifteenth-century gargoyle."

"Sounds like the only reasonable course of action to me." Grinning, Bittersohn took the phone. "Hello, X-9? This is 007. How can I get in there without being caught? Coal chute, right. Sure, you bet. Nine o'clock on the dot. Roger, over and out."

He slammed down the receiver. "Madam, can you equip an expedition? Brooks wants ham sandwiches and root beer. He didn't say anything about hanging a lantern aloft in the belfry arch, but I don't suppose it would hurt."

"One moment there, my fine Hairbreadth Harry. Why nine o' clock?"

"Because they're having some kind of shindig there that's supposed to be over by eight and may drag on till half-past, and Brooks figures the fun won't start until the coast is clear. So that gives me time enough to eat my dinner like a *mensch* before I descend the coal chute."

"In those good clothes?"

"Nay, fair maiden. I shall wear my chute-shooting suit. How about, in the immortal words of Bobbie Burns, ae fond kiss before we sever?" He didn't wait for her answer.

She struggled free at last. "Unhand me, sir! That embrace was obtained under false pretenses. What makes you think we're severing?"

"Sarah, you can't go. It might be dangerous."

"In the immortal words of Carrie Jacobs Bond, big deal! I was in danger of arrest for indecent exposure the day you made me wear that sari, and a fat lot you cared. I was in danger of being seduced by Bill Jones last night – "

"Were you indeed?"

"Indeed I was, or might have been. He invited me to his pad while we were having that drink. I only managed to save myself by declining with thanks."

"Did you have to thank him?"

"It seemed the courteous thing to do. He was paying for the drinks. Just think, if I'd accepted, he wouldn't have let the boys use his pad and he wouldn't have had to seek solace with Lydia, poor thing. She's still hanging on, by the way. I just spoke with the nurse. Now nip down to the corner and get Brooks his root beer while I break the news to Mrs. Sorpende that she's being stood up."

Mrs. Sorpende took the blow bravely, making reference to the fact that when duty whispers low, 'Thou must,' the youth replies, 'I can,' and expressing the opinion that Mr. Brooks Kelling showed a delight-fully youthful exuberance of spirit. Sarah had to agree even as she wondered what further mess her cousin's exuberance was about to get them into.

After dinner she retired to her bedroom promptly on the half-hour, put on an old pair of pants and a jacket she usually wore for things like cleaning out the gutters at Ireson's Landing. She sneaked down the back stairs, collected Brooks's ham sand-wiches, root beer, and a bottle opener from the kitchen, and met Bittersohn by stealth in the back alley. He had his car and they lost no time getting to the palazzo. Precisely at nine, they were crouched in front of a small oblong window set into the foundation of the palazzo and conveniently screened by a high privet hedge.

"This is it, my love," Bittersohn poked at the sash and the window swung noiselessly inward. "I'd better go first to catch you in case there's a big drop at the bottom. Are you sure you can manage?"

"Don't be ridiculous," Sarah told him scornfully. "I'd go down belly-bumper if it weren't for the root beer."

"The hell you would." He inserted his long legs in the small aperture, lay flat, and vanished into blackness. Sarah heard a swish, a thud, then a muffled "Next, please."

Sarah poked her feet through as he had, murmured hysterically, "If Cousin Mabel could only see me now!" took a firmer grip on the sandwich bag, and shoved off.

A second later Bittersohn had her in his arms, root beer and all. "Are you okay?" he whispered.

"Yes, fine. Where's Brooks?"

"Right here," hissed her cousin. "Did you bring the sandwiches?"

"Yes, and a rousing Godspeed from Mrs. Sorpende, though she's sorry to miss the angleworms. Are you starved?"

"Ravenous, but I don't care to eat in the coalbin. Too gritty. Follow me and don't make a sound."

Walking flat on the soles of his feet, Indian style, Brooks led his cohorts up the basement stairs, through the Donatello Wing, and straight toward the Grand Staircase. "We'll have to risk it," he breathed. "There's no other way."

"Where are we going?" whispered Bittersohn.

"Third floor. Sh-h!"

He shoved them into the refuge of an alleged cathedral stall as footsteps pounded toward them on the tiled floor. The watchman passed within six feet of them and vanished through the door to the basement they'd just left.

"Timed that just right." Brooks chuckled softly. "Now we make a dash for it. Keep close to the balustrade."

He charged upward like Great-uncle Nathan Kelling at San Juan Hill, Max and Sarah at his heels. They reached the Titian Room without incident. "And now," said Brooks in hushed but firm tones, "let's have those sandwiches. We're safe for exactly sixteen minutes and thirty-two seconds. Ah, I see you remembered the bottle opener. Anyone for root beer?"

"I'd rather have a clue as to what this is all about," said Bittersohn.

"So should I," Brooks replied through a mouthful of ham. "I can only tell you that Dr. Aguinaldo Ruy Lopez was back again this afternoon in a different guise. Casing the joint, I believe it's called. He had an odd-looking chap with him and from an injudicious word this other fellow let drop in my hearing I deduced they were plotting to break in tonight. I don't know what they're up to, but whatever it is will apparently take place here in the Titian Room."

He refreshed himself with a swig of root beer and deployed his forces. "Sarah, you get back into that sedan chair out in the Grand Salon. Maintain a vigilant lookout. As soon as you detect any sign of activity on the stairs, put your hand up to the rear window and wave this handkerchief of mine. It has a luminous monogram. Bittersohn, you lurk behind that suit of spurious medieval armor in the corner by the door."

"*Oui, mon capitaine.* Where will you be?"

"Up there." Brooks pointed to the massive overhanging hood of a fifteenth-century Italian fireplace.

"You'll kill yourself," Sarah protested.

"No, I shan't. I did a test run this afternoon." He swarmed up the carvings like a middle-aged rhesus monkey. "Can you see me?"

"You blend in with the decor."

"Good. Now, you both understand what you're to do?"

"No. What happens when they get here?"

"We rely on the inspiration of the moment. Would you mind handing me up another sandwich?"

"I hope they don't track us down by the odor of delicatessen," Sarah muttered.

"No fear of that with ham, I believe. Pastrami would have presented a risk. Now, if I may just have what's left of the root beer? Good girl. Take the bag with you into the sedan chair and mind you don't rattle the paper. Places, everyone."

Saran scuttled back to the sedan chair and settled herself in the same place where she'd struggled to pin her sari back on, praying that the dust in the cushions wouldn't make her sneeze at the wrong moment. As the eternities ticked by, she realized she could have sneezed her head off and it wouldn't have mattered. After an aeon or two, the watchman trudged by on his rounds, not even bothering to glance at the chair. Sarah reached stealthily into the bag, extracted the last ham sandwich, and ate it.

At least it was fairly warm in the chair, and the seat wasn't too hard. What with the stuffiness and her exhaustion from the previous night's activities, she was having a hard time keeping her eyes open. She relaxed against the musty cushions for just a moment, felt herself slipping off the seat, and sat up with a jerk. Had she actually dropped off to sleep? Poor Max must be having screaming fidgets by now.

Then she heard a clatter on the stairs and a voice from somewhere below saying, "Like I told you, man, it's a breeze."

CHAPTER 22

Sarah held Cousin Brooks's luminous monogram to the dusty glass and waved frantically, though surely the two lurkers in the Titian Room must have heard the commotion on the stairs, too. The invaders were making no effort to be quiet. They must know they had nothing to fear from the watchman. Either they'd tied him up or – Sarah hoped to heaven they'd only tied him up.

She saw a yellowish glow from some sort of light they were carrying. Now she could tell who they both were. One was Lupe, as she'd expected. The other was Bengo, the painter who'd fluffed Rembrandt's cat. Bengo was staggering under the weight of what looked like a huge suitcase. Lupe bristled with an assortment of long, slender, rodlike objects with blobs on their ends. Were they planning to erect an abstract sculpture? Was this merely some far-out joke?

No, they wouldn't be doing a thing like this just for fun. Lupe wasn't that sort. And they were going into the Titian Room, as Brooks had thought they would. Following the dim light, Sarah could make out a shadow detaching itself from the suit of armor in the corner and sneaking after the two. Her heart froze. All she could think was, "I must love him terribly. I couldn't be this scared if I didn't."

What if they had guns? What if Cousin Brooks took a notion to leap Tarzan-like from the medieval carvings and capture them, and failed? Sarah remembered all too well what Joe Witherspoon's body looked like falling past her eyes to land among the hyacinths. But the gargoyles all stayed put and she began to relax a bit.

Whatever were they up to in there? She could hear thuds, crashes, altercations in an outdated gibberish that consisted mostly of the words "like," "man," and "dig." She could see that yellowish light bobbing around. It must be an ordinary flashlight with something tied over the lens to make the gleam less noticeable from outside. Gradually curiosity got the better of caution. Sarah opened the well-oiled door inch by inch and eased herself out of the sedan chair. Her foot struck the paper bag and she pulled back in terror, but the rattle of paper must have been too faint to be heard above the racket Lupe and Bengo were making.

She wasn't the only one who'd got tired of sitting still. Slowly, noiselessly, one of the effigies was moving down off that towering mantel. Cousin Brooks had once remarked that he could get within two feet of a hermit thrush, shyest of birds, without causing it to twitch a tailfeather. Now she believed him. Well, if he was getting into the action, so was she.

Grateful for her dark clothes, old sneakers, and the obscuring veil of coal dust she must have acquired on her way down the chute, she slithered into the Titian Room. Brooks neither turned his head nor made any start of surprise, but reached out for her elbow and steered her into the shadow of the immense carved fireplace. Now she had a ringside view of the action.

The Titian Room was being tranformed into a photography studio. The bulbous objects turned out to be floodlights on metal tripods. They had been set up in a semicircle around the huge "Rape of Lucrece." A professional box camera that must have been in the big case stood in front of the painting. At the moment Lupe's head was under a black viewing cloth and Bengo was holding the hooded flashlight to illuminate the canvas.

Now Lupe's head emerged from under the cloth. "Okay, man, we're in focus. Now you see why we boosted this stuff from the camera store?"

"Man, you got smarts like it's goin' out of style," Bengo replied in awe and reverence. "How you get all them brains in one skull, like?"

"You an operator, you operate. Now, man, we get us some feelthy peectures in like living color of this fat broad with the big boobs. Then you paint us a copy on that big canvas we been antiquing out on Leroy's roof."

"I dig, man. Then we sell the copy."

"No, man. Then we come back here with the copy, put it in the frame like, and boost us a genuine Titian."

"Cat daddy," breathed Bengo, "you are ba-ad!"

"Man, I hear you talkin'. Now plug in them lights an' like watch the birdie."

"What if the fuzz spot the lights through the window?"

"Who cares? We be long gone while the fuzz still huntin' for the doorknob.

Like plug 'em in, man."

"Like where?"

"Like in the outlets. Ain't you got no smarts?"

"Man, I got no outlets."

"What you mean, no outlets? Even Leroy's pad got outlets."

Brooks pulled Sarah closer to the fireplace as the conspirators' flashlight made a frantic circuit of the baseboards and walls. She could feel his wiry little body shaking, and thought at first he was having an attack of nerves. Then she realized her cousin was overcome with silent hilarity, and she remembered why.

When the palazzo was erected, Madam Wilkins had reluctantly installed a coal furnace as a necessary concession to the rigors of Boston winters. In other respects, she'd been a stickler for authenticity. The Medici didn't have electric lights and she wasn't having them either.

Brooks got himself under control at last, cleared his throat, and stepped out into the light. "Bengo is quite right, Dr. Ruy Lopez. There are no outlets. But don't worry. I came prepared."

The explosion of his miniature flash gun caught the pair open-mouthed. Bittersohn

287

leaped out of the gloom and grabbed them in a double armlock. Lupe struggled in vain to get free. Bengo, however, had not bathed in many moons. His skin was so greasy that he managed to slither away.

"Get that camera," yelled Lupe.

Sarah shrieked as Bengo made a dive for Brooks, but that resourceful gentleman merely stuck out his foot. His attacker sprawled flat on the authentic Venetian flagstone floor. She picked up the dropped flashlight, stripped off the old sock that covered the lens, and gave them a better light. Now she could see Max Bittersohn holding Lupe six inches off the floor and shaking him into passivity. Brooks was seated comfortably on Bengo's shoulder blades, holding out a little box of safety matches.

"Be a good girl, Sarah, and light the candles in those sconces. We may as well have some illumination as we chat over the events of the evening."

"I ain't rattin'," Bengo gasped.

"I am," said Lupe. "Anything you gentlemen want to know, I be happy to sing like the dinkey bird in the amfalula tree. Maybe we could like work out a deal."

"You're in no position to deal." Bittersohn gave Lupe a final shake and set him down with a thump.

At last the dealer was able to get a look at the man who'd caught him. "You?" he gasped. "Fuzz? Man, that ain't cricket."

"Tough toenails, cat daddy. Now talk. Who put you up to this?"

"Nobody, man."

"Are you quite sure?"

"Man, if I had somebody to rat on, you think I wouldn't? It was like inspiration. It just come over me, man."

"While you were playing Dr. Aguinaldo Ruy Lopez to make a sucker out of Max Bittersohn, right?"

Lupe smiled and said nothing.

"Who hired you for the Ruy Lopez act?"

"What's in it for me if I tell?"

"There might be quite a lot of you don't."

"Man, you don't have to get nasty. I said I'd sing, didn't I? It was Lunchless."

"Lunchless who?"

"Like Lunchless. Man, you know. The fat old cat with the notes. Bernie's babysitter."

"Are you referring to Nicholas Fieringer, who arranges the concerts Bernie plays in?"

"Man, what I just say? Lunchless comes up to me and says, how I like to make half a yard? I say I like it fine. Like green is my favoritest color, man."

"Did Fieringer tell you why you were to do this impersonation?"

"Man, who needs to know? Anybody offer me long bread to wash my neck and speak Spanish for a while I don't ask no questions, man."

"Even though it meant coming to the place where your uncle had just been murdered?"

Lupe shrugged. "Man, you got to pick it where it grows."

"What made you think of reversing your customary procedure and selling an original instead of a copy?"

"I tell you, man, it just come to me."

"Didn't it occur to you that you might have problems fencing a hot Titian?"

"Man, we got sporting goods dealers in this town could fence *Old Ironsides*."

"Like who?"

"I look around. I find somebody."

"Perhaps your uncle could have helped you if he hadn't been bumped off down in that locker room, where I assume you killed the watchman."

"Man, I never hit nobody. That ain't my thing, man. We just tie him up and lock him in the can, like."

"You'd better be telling the truth about

that. Whom was your uncle working for?"

"Like I tell you, man, who needs to know?"

"I do, for one. When did your uncle tell you what was going on around here?"

"Man, he tell me nothin'."

"Too bad. You could have profited from the information."

"Like how?" said Lupe eagerly.

"Like for instance you might have learned this genuine Titian you were planning to boost had already been boosted. Like this is a fake, man."

From under the seated Brooks, Bengo raised his head to gaze up at his captive leader. "Man," he said, "you are ba-ad!"

CHAPTER 23

"Palmerston hasn't a prayer of hushing up the stolen painting story now," said Bittersohn with justifiable satisfaction. He and Sarah were on their way back to Tulip Street, having left Brooks and the watchman, who had indeed been found irate but unharmed in the sanitary facility, to turn over the prisoners and reap the glory.

"I know," Sarah replied drowsily. "Lupe will rat all over the place. He seems to think that someone else's having stolen the Titian before he could makes him an innocent victim. What will they do to him, I wonder?"

"Charge him with breaking and entering with assault and intent to commit grand larceny." Bittersohn's words were half stifled by a jaw-cracking yawn. "With his connections he'll probably beat the rap somehow."

"He'll claim Bengo forced him into it."

"No doubt. Well, here's the old homestead. Tired, sweetie pumpkin?"

"Absolutely beat, though not in Lupe's sense of the word. These middle-aged hippie types give one a feeling of *déjà vu,* don't they? I can remember my mother fussing about their fornicating on the sidewalks and getting furious with me when I asked her what fornicating meant. Oh, dear, someone just turned on the light in the library. I told Charles not to wait up."

But Charles was at the door before Sarah could get her key in the lock, looking dashing as all get-out in a Noel Coward lounging robe.

"Hail to thee, blithe spirit," said Bittersohn. "What's up besides you?"

"The hospital informs me that Countess Ouspenska has regained consciousness."

"Damn! I shouldn't have put the car away."

"We can't go at this hour," Sarah protested. "They won't let us in."

"Yes they will. I did the director a favor once."

"You and your connections! All right, Charles, call us a cab."

"You do not intend to visit the Massachusetts General Hospital in those clothes, madam?" the butler said frostily.

"Why not?"

"You and Mr. Bittersohn both look, if I may take the liberty of saying so, as if you've been crawling around a coal-bin."

"Come to think of it, we have. Five minutes, then."

A quick wash and change revived them both somewhat. A quarter of an hour later, hollow-eyed but presentable, they were getting a cool reception from a night nurse and being led into the private room Bittersohn had wangled for Countess Ouspenska.

Lydia looked ghastly. Gray skin was stretched so tight over her high cheekbones that it seemed about to split open from the strain. Her eyes were deep black pits and her mouth a slate blue gash. Still she tried to smile. "The beautiful ones," she whispered. "I am some party-pooper, not?"

Sarah kissed the ashen cheeks and took the ice-cold hands in her own. "We're so terribly grateful that you're — " She checked herself. If Lydia didn't realize how close to death she'd been, this was hardly the time to tell her. "We'll have another party as soon as you're well enough to come."

"Is good. I be there with bells on."

"Sure you will, Lydia," said Bittersohn, self-conscious as men often are in sickrooms. He pulled up a chair and pushed Sarah gently into it. "Have they told you what happened?"

"They say, how come I do such crazy thing? What crazy thing I do, Max?"

"They think you fed yourself a mixture of arsenic and Nembutal playing Russian roulette with your stomach capsules."

"But not! Never I do such a thing. That was for leg-pull to make sputter the good Dolores. Does she say I take poison?"

"She said you told her you were going to."

"Is like Dolores to believe when I joke. No imagination. Must be hell to be artist with no imagination." Lydia was still obviously very sick. Showing no curiosity about her own dreadful experience, she rambled on.

"Ever since I know Dolores is many years now she works, always she works. When not at Madam's dusting ugly china is painting in studio with door locked nobody should breathe on masterpieces. I say, 'Show me what great thing you create always painting, painting.' She show me still life with dead bird. Not even live bird to whistle while she work. Is always still life never finished. I tease about it only yesterday. Is yesterday? I forget when I — " Her voice faded and the nurse made them leave the room.

"She's right about that painting," Sarah remarked. "Dolores had it on the easel the day I went there for tea. Max, do you suppose – ?"

"Let's go." Bittersohn overawed the nurse with some precise and frightening instructions, then dragged Sarah to the elevators.

"How could I have been such an idiot?" Sarah wailed. "It's been sticking out all over the place. Dolores is an expert copyist. She showed me photographs of some portraits that she'd copied from other photographs and you could hardly tell which was which. And she had every opportunity to get the paintings in and out of the museum. She'd need only say she was taking the original to her studio for revarnishing or whatever, then return the copy instead."

"I thought of her first off the bat," said Bittersohn shamefacedly, "but she was so damned obvious I couldn't believe it was that easy. Besides, those thick ankles sort of throw you off."

"I know. She's the salt of the earth. Is this the lobby? Max, do you see what I see?"

A trim little man with slicked-down gray hair was sitting near the main entrance.

"Hello, brighteyes," said Max.

"Good morning, children," Cousin Brooks replied. "I called your private number, Bittersohn, to tell you Lupe and Bengo had been safely jugged, and Charles answered. He said you were over here, so I came along. I was just down around the corner at the jail anyway. How's Lydia?"

"Groggy but recovering. So you got the lads tucked in for the night."

"Unless Lupe managed to talk his way out by now, which wouldn't surprise me. What's next on the agenda?"

"We were about to pay a call on Dolores Tawne. Incidentally, Kelling, I hope you're not – er – "

"Emotionally involved with her? Not in the least. As a matter of fact" – Cousin Brooks smirked tenderly into the night as they emerged in quest of yet another cab – "I've come to the conclusion that my affections are engaged elsewhere. Like the Canada goose I'm monogamous by nature. I've avoided entanglements until such time as I felt ready to mate for life. But now I'm all set to be netted and banded."

"Congratulations. When does the mating season begin?"

"I don't know. I haven't broached the subject to Theonia yet.'

"Don't you think she should be among the first to know?" said Sarah.

"Dash it, I'm going to pop the question as soon as I get a chance to do it properly. I can't just pounce on her like a hawk on a chicken."

"Why not? She'd love being swept off her feet."

"Too bad there aren't more like her," said Bittersohn, sweeping Sarah off her feet and into the taxi that stopped for them. "Has it ever crossed your mind, Kelling, that Dolores Tawne may be responsible for all those fakes at the Madam's?"

"Dolores? Are you serious? She couldn't—but she could, couldn't she? That opens up a rather startling train of thought. If she is, I must be an accessory either before or after the fact. I must have copied at least thirty of the Wilkins's frames for her. She always claims she wants them to put on portraits she's painted."

"Have you seen any of the portraits?"

"As a matter of fact, no. She never offers and I never ask. The only work of hers I've ever seen was an unfinished still life she was working on I don't know how many years ago. It has a stuffed pheasant in it that was as ridiculously incompetent a job of taxidermy as it's ever been my misfortune to encounter. I pointed out its defects and she got into a snit. I've always assumed that's why she hasn't shown me any more."

"Would you testify in court to her having asked you to copy the frames?"

"I hope I know my civic duty, Bittersohn. Drat! This reminds me of the first time I ever saw a scarlet tanager in molt. One would have sworn that all of a sudden it belonged to a different subspecies." Brooks shook his neat head sadly and didn't speak again until they'd reached their now familiar destination at Ipswich Street.

For the second night in a row they were treated to the sight of Mrs. Tawne in her plissé robe and metal curlers. She was even more annoyed this time.

"Oh, it's you, Brooks," she sniffed. "I must say I thought you knew enough to show consideration for others even if your fine young lady cousin and her paramour don't. What is it this time?"

"We came to congratulate you," said the paramour, "on the magnificent job you've done copying all those paintings at the Wilkins Museum."

Bittersohn expected a reaction but not the one he got. Dolores almost kissed him.

"Why, thank you, Mr. Bittersohn! I must say that's sweet music to my ears coming from a man of your professional reputation. I'm sorry I was a bit short with you just now. I had no idea — but come in, come in. I'll put the kettle on. It won't take a second."

And off she rushed, leaving the art expert agape on the doorstep. Sarah gave him a poke. "Go on, you idiot!" She herself led the way down from the balcony, making polite tea party noises. The men sat on the edges of chairs and looked stunned while Dolores did things in the kitchen.

In a few minutes she was back loaded with food and apologizing for the meagerness of the entertainment. "If I'd known you were coming I'd have had something on hand. Do try the chocolate marshmallow coconut fluffs, Mr. Bittersohn."

Max blenched and helped himself to a plain cracker. "Thanks, I'll start with this," he muttered.

"We know we shouldn't have barged in on you so late," Sarah gushed, "but we've been at the hospital with Countess Ouspenska. She's coming along nicely and we thought you'd want to know."

Dolores merely inclined her curlers and

smiled vaguely. "That's good. Now, about my paintings, Mr. Bittersohn. You don't know what it means to me to be complimented by a truly discerning person. If I say so myself," and she did say so herself, pausing only to refill cups and press more goodies on her stupefied audience. The amount of technical data she reeled off was amazing. It became evident that Dolores was an authority on the duplication of old masters, that she was immensely proud of her ability, and that she saw nothing improper in what she'd done. All she regretted was the need for anonymity.

"An artist does appreciate recognition," she sighed. "So many times I've stood there listening to visitors rave over my work and fairly had to bite my tongue to keep from letting them know they weren't looking at a Rubens or a Rembrandt but a Dolores Agnew Tawne. Ah well, it isn't every painter who gets mistaken for Rembrandt." She chuckled and helped herself to another chocolate marshmallow coconut fluff.

"You needn't worry about the lack of recognition," said Bittersohn. "I predict that before long this place will be full of television cameras and your name will be in every newspaper in the country."

"Wouldn't that be something!" Their

hostess gazed dreamily over the top of her cookie. "But I'm afraid it won't happen till I'm long past caring. Absolute secrecy is our watchword, as of course you know."

"Yes, we've had that forcibly impressed upon us."

"I must say I'm surprised he told you three, though of course I knew he'd been in contact with you. I suppose he was more or less forced to reveal all on account of Witherspoon and Brown. That was an odd coincidence, I must admit. I'd never have thought Brown was so devoted to poor old Joe, but who knows what secrets lurk in the hearts of men, as the Shadow used to say. I've been on pins and needles ever since Sunday. We've always been worried for fear something would happen that might lead to somebody's questioning the authenticity of the copies, not that there's much likelihood, if I do say so myself. Still, as he's often said to me, if the wrong people got hold of the information out motives could be most unpleasantly distorted. Some folks are always ready to believe the worst, you know."

CHAPTER 24

Sarah took a shot in the dark. "Ah, but outsiders don't know you as we do, Mrs. Tawne. Once you were given the opportunity to explain, I'm sure there could be no misunderstanding. I've been sitting here wondering how you yourself would sum up the overall program in simple laymen's terms."

"Why, I honestly hadn't thought. I never expected to be called upon to make the announcement." Dolores was clearly flattered by the suggestion.

"But why shouldn't you? I personally don't think it's quite fair for you to have been kept so entirely out of the limelight all this time. Do you, Mr. Bittersohn?"

"I certainly don't," said Max. "Do you, Kelling?"

"I don't understand it at all," said Brooks with simple truth. "You've never impressed me as any shrinking violet, Dolores."

"I hope I can put public duty before mere

personal vanity, Brooks. No, I'm not going to make any formal disclosure until I receive his instructions to do so. I've done whatever he told me to without question for thirty-two years. Far be it from me to step in and try to hog the glory now that our great work is so near completion."

"What do you mean, our?" said Brooks. "You've just been telling us you did them all yourself."

"Every single brushstroke on every one of those great masterpieces is mine and mine alone," said the artist with fierce pride, "but he has always emphasized that we work as a team. 'You do the work and I bear the responsibility,' he says. And I'm proud to reveal that in spite of the countless demands on his time and energies, his interest has never flagged. Never for one second."

Dolores waxed oratorical. "I can truthfully say that without his faith and trust, his continuing support and inspiration, I could never have accomplished what I did. When I faltered, he spurred me on. 'I know you will not let our great work down,' he has said time and again. Through him I have found the strength to fulfill my mission."

"Bravo," cried Bittersohn. "By the way, Mrs. Tawne, I hope Mr. C. Edwald Palmerston has expressed his appreciation – er –materially as well as verbally."

"He has been as generous as the limitations of the museum's budget will allow," said Dolores stiffly, "and more. In fact he pays for every cent's worth of my art materials out of his own pocket. His own pocket. I'll bet he didn't tell you that."

"No," Bittersohn replied, "he didn't."

"That's so like him. 'Do good by stealth,' that's his motto. I daresay he didn't even mention that he also pays for maintaining the vault."

"I can't believe this."

"It's absolutely true. And it must be a pretty penny, what with the temperature and humidity controls and the hermetic sealing and all that, not to mention the initial cost of construction."

"Eh?" snapped Brooks, "what's that?"

"Why surely he explained about the vault. That's the whole cornerstone of our work. That," Dolores was orating again, "is the overwhelming responsibility Mr. Palmerston took upon himself when he first became chairman of the board of trustees. Madam Wilkins's original purchase is preserved against the ravages of time, climate, and environmental pollution under scientifically controlled conditions in a dustproof, bomb-proof, radiationproof, mothproof vault, while a perfect copy is displayed to the public. It wouldn't do, of course," she explained in a more matter-of-fact tone, "to come straight out and say the paintings are copies, so we've quietly substituted them one by one as I've finished the duplications, and nobody has been the wiser. Never once in thirty-two years has anybody raised a question."

A shadow flickered across her functional countenance. "That is, nobody ever did until that old fool Joe Witherspoon started moaning about his sweetheart's having changed. It was right after we changed the paintings, I'll grant you that, but there's no way Joe could have found out. That Titian I consider my master-piece. I'll bet I worked harder on the copy than Titian himself did on the original, and if you can find one single flaw anywhere, I'll eat my palette."

"The Titian is the museum's most valuable possession, right?" said Bittersohn.

"Oh, yes. Far and away the gem of the collection. We left it till almost the last because to tell you the truth, we were almost afraid to tackle it. It's so big, and it's a painting that really gets looked at, if you know what I mean. Mr. Palmerston was nervous as a cat on hot bricks. 'You must positively outdo yourself this time,' he kept telling me."

"And you did, Mrs. Tawne. It's remarkable that Witherspoon managed to spot the substitution."

"He did no such thing! Joe was getting soft in the head from old age, that's all."

"Did Mr. Palmerston know Joe was telling the other guards that the painting had been altered?"

"There's precious little goes on around the palazzo that Mr. Palmerston doesn't know. Certainly he knew. I told him myself."

"Then it must have been something of a relief to you both, if I may say so, when Witherspoon took that header off the balcony."

"I'm frank to say I didn't shed many tears when I heard the news, though I didn't relish the adverse publicity for the museum. And when I found out that darn fool Brown had made a bad matter worse with his clowning around pretending to have been robbed, I almost had a fit. Of all the times to pick! If I'd been there when it happened, I don't say but what I might have been tempted to toss him after old Joe and be done with the pair of them."

"But you weren't in the palazzo then?"

"No, I wasn't. If you must know, I was over at Jimmy's place putting ice packs on his head so he'd be in some kind of shape to go to work Monday. I'm afraid it's no great secret that my brother gets a bit above himself now and then. He'd got hold of a few extra dollars Saturday night and gone on a bender unbeknownst to me. If I'd found out in time he had the money – "

"Where did it come from?"

"As a matter of fact, Mr. Palmerston gave it to him in a moment of forgetfulness. Jimmy does odd jobs for him sometimes and he always insists on paying, though I've told him over and over I wish he wouldn't."

"Doesn't he know your brother will drink up the money as soon as he gets it?"

"I suppose he keeps hoping Jimmy will reform," sighed Mrs. Tawne. "Being such a pillar of rectitude himself, he doesn't always take into consideration the weaknesses of others. He's been very understanding about Jimmy, by and large. Mr. Palmerston is one of the world's real philanthropists."

Sarah thought of another experiment to try. "He more or less gave us to understand that the vault had been your idea."

Dolores beamed. "Isn't that just like him!

No, it was entirely his own personal inspiration. Of course I advised him on the details," she added quickly.

"You also picked out the location, I believe?"

"Not I. Strange as it may seem, I don't even know where the vault is situated. He always has felt that it best that I remain totally aloof from that part of the project. 'You have enough on your shoulders as it is,' he tells me. 'I must not burden you with any unnecessary responsibility.' He understands the immense pressures the creative artist is subjected to."

"Then you've never even visited the vault?"

"Never."

"You just bring a painting here and copy it, then he takes away the original and that's the last you see of it."

"That's it in a nutshell, Mrs. Kelling. Of course I don't keep the originals here all the time I'm working on them. What I do is take pictures and make sketches and careful notes, then I work mostly from those. Since I have my own keys to the palazzo, I can always run over during off-hours and make a comparison if I have to. When the time comes to make a substitution, sometimes I do that, sometimes he does. If it's a really important one like the Titian, we do it together."

"And that's all there is to it?"

"Well, not quite." Dolores actually simpered. "After the job is done, we meet back here and have a little private celebration. I fix us a nice snack, Mr. Palmerston brings a bottle of champagne, and we drink a toast to the success of our enterprise. Then he delivers a brief address about how future generations will be grateful to us for preserving their priceless heritage from the ravages of time and so on. Of course there's nobody but me to hear the speeches, more's the pity. I've suggested making tape recordings to put in the vault with the paintings, but he won't hear of it. True greatness and true modesty go hand in hand, as I've often told him."

That was too much for Brooks Kelling. "True horsefeathers," he snorted. "That old goat's been pulling the wool over your eyes for thirty-two years and you're too damned infatuated to admit it."

"I'll thank you to explain that remark, Brooks Kelling," said Mrs. Tawne dangerously.

Bittersohn intervened. "Perhaps this will explain better than Kelling can." He showed her Bill Jones's list, now tattered from much handling. "If you'll check over this listing, Mrs. Tawne, you'll see where, when, and for approximately how much money each one of the originals you copied was sold."

Dolores stared at the paper. "But – but this is crazy! They're all in the vault."

"The vault you've never seen and don't know where to look for? I'm afraid that vault exists only in C. Edwald Palmerston's imagination, Mrs. Tawne."

"In other words, Dolores," said Brooks cruelly, "you've been led up the garden path."

"I don't believe you. He couldn't. He wouldn't! Mr. Palmerston is a fine, noble, philanthropic gentleman."

"Like hell he is."

"And besides" – the woman's anguished bewilderment was pathetic – "why would he do such a dreadful thing to me?"

"For money," Bittersohn told her.

"Mr. Palmerston doesn't need money. He's a rich man. He gives lavishly to worthy causes."

"He certainly does, and it's never cost him a cent. One might add that Mr. Palmerston has other expensive philanthropies."

"Such as?"

"Women, mostly."

"Women? Oh, no. Not Mr. Palmerston."

"I'm afraid you don't know the man as well as you think you do, Mrs. Tawne. He's kept you slaving for thirty-two years in order to support a series of expensive lady friends."

"Who for instance?" Dolores had fight in her still. "If you mean that Ouspenska trollop – "

"She was one, yes. When she was young and beautiful, of course. That's how he likes them. Doesn't he, Mrs. Kelling?"

Bittersohn gave Sarah a surreptitious poke. With downcast eyes, she followed his cue.

"You must remember, Mrs. Tawne, that I'd led a very sheltered life. I simply didn't understand what he was leading up to until – well, how could any silly young girl have resisted? Orchids every day, lavish dinners, sables, weekend flights to Monte Carlo – "

"You're lying," said Dolores faintly. "This is all some insane joke."

"Mrs. Tawne, does a betrayed woman lie about such things?" Sarah covered her face with her hands.

"How – how many others – ?"

Sarah shrugged wearily. "I couldn't say. I doubt whether he could, either."

"And all of them – orchids, jewels, sables, trips to Monte Carlo?"

"Lately I believe it's been Tahiti."

"Tahiti? And me painting my guts out for a bottle of cheap champagne once or twice a year?"

Dolores Tawne turned brick red, then chalk white. She sank back in her chair and stared blindly at the paint-stained floor of her studio. "You're right, Brooks," she said. "I'm nothing but a damned old fool."

CHAPTER 25

Dolores would have confronted Palmerston in curlers and kimono if Brooks hadn't told her to act her age and get some clothes on. She was still fuming like a volcano about to erupt when she led the charge up C. Edwald's elegant brownstone steps.

A pretty young maid in a sexy negligee answered the doorbell, and that capped the climax. Aflame with righteous ire, Mrs. Tawne steamed to the attack with Max and Brooks at her heels and the maid trailing behind wringing her hands and bleating questions to which none of them paid any attention.

Sarah missed the first part of the confrontation because Bittersohn had commanded her to find a telephone and get hold of Fitzpatrick and Fitzgibbon. When she reached the scene of battle, easily located by the stridencies in which Dolores Tawne's voice led all the rest, Palmerston was sitting up in bed, prudishly clutching an eiderdown to his chin with one hand and groping for his teeth and eyeglasses with the other, gummily and ineffectually trying to defend himself.

"But, Mrs. Tawne," he mumbled, "my motives were wholly humanitarian."

"Humanitarian my backside!" shrieked his enraged dupe. "Buying sable coats for that little tramp right there, I don't doubt."

The maid burst into loud sobs. "It's only m-muskrat."

"There, see!"

"Now, Dolores – "

"Don't you Dolores me! I've never been one of your fancy pieces and you can't try to make out I have. Just because I don't paint my face and wear dresses cut down to my b-bellybutton – " She, too, started to cry.

Bittersohn put her gently aside. "You might as well come clean, Palmerston. The police are on their way here. Lydia Ouspenska has survived the dose of arsenic and Nembutal you put in her stomach capsule. She's awake and talking. Mrs. Tawne's going to spill all she knows about your faked painting racket, and we already have Bill Jones's testimony about how and when and where you got rid of the paintings, so I daresay one or two of the fences will be willing to finger you in exchange for immunity from prosecution. Perhaps Mrs. Tawne can also tell us about an unfinished Murillo that turned up in Ouspenska's studio all of a sudden last night."

"Is that where it went?" gasped Dolores. "He sent Nick Fieringer to get it last night. I couldn't imagine why. I warned Nick to be awfully careful about the wet paint. I hope he was."

"He was," said Bittersohn. "Too bad you were so conscientious, Mrs. Tawne, or we might have got along a little faster. As to why the painting was moved, I expect it was an attempt to make the countess look like the person who'd been painting the fakes. She was supposed to die, you see. Palmerston thought, no doubt, that she was already dead by then and wouldn't be able to correct the misapprehension. You told him her Russian roulette joke, didn't you?"

"Yes. Yes, I told him. And he'd have robbed me of the credit for thirty-two years' work to save his own rotten skin?"

"Why not? He'd robbed just about everything else there was to rob by then, and things were getting a bit warm around the Madam's. He had to get out from under somehow, didn't he? Otherwise the world might lose one of its real philanthropists. By the way, Palmerston, Nick Fieringer will be talking, too. He's already explained how you got him to hire Dr. Aguinaldo Ruy Lopez, whom your man Kelling here had the pleasure of seeing safely to jail about an hour ago. Fieringer can tell the police about that Murillo and the phial of arsenic you got him to plant in Ouspenska's bureau drawer."

Palmerston's lips twitched and Bittersohn noticed. "I see. You planted the arsenic yourself the night you took Lydia home from Mrs. Kelling's. That's a minor detail. We know you gave Jimmy Agnew money Saturday night so that he'd get drunk and be absent from work on Sunday and you'd have an easier chance to hide in that sedan chair on the balcony without being noticed. You must have been rather upset with your faithful friend and confidante Mrs. Tawne for being able to produce a substitute guard at such short notice, but you went ahead and you were lucky. You'd arranged with Brown to get Witherspoon on the balcony somehow so that you could nip out and shove him over the railing. You anticipated a hue and cry, and you ordered Brown to fake an assault and attempted robbery in the

317

chapel so that attention would be drawn away from the Grand Salon and you could make a getaway. The next day you killed Brown to shut him up by putting paint remover and a pinch of rat poison in his whiskey bottle."

"I deny everything," shouted Palmerston.

"And a fat lot of good that's going to do you," said Brooks Kelling. "You remembered to wipe your fingerprints off the paint remover bottle, but you forgot about the rat poison and I found it under my workbench."

Palmerston at last managed to get his teeth in, and bared them ferociously at the substitute guard. "Kelling," he snarled, "you're fired."

Fitzpatrick and Fitzgibbon had now arrived. They took a bit of convincing before they would consent to carry so august a person as C. Edwald Palmerston off to be booked for grand larceny, murder, attempted murder, and betrayal of the public trust, but Bittersohn convinced them.

What with one thing and another it was almost dawn by the time Sarah, Max, and Brooks got back to Tulip Street. Since Brooks had reasonable qualms about disturbing his own landlady at such an hour, Sarah offered him the hospitality of the library couch. They were all three very late getting up. Only Mrs. Sorpende was left at the breakfast table by the time they appeared. She deserved an explanation and she got one.

"I can't get over it," Sarah mused when the outlines had been filled in. "When I think of all the times Palmerston upstaged Great-uncle Frederick with those huge donations to the Home for Delinquent Dowagers and so forth!"

"Not to mention the sables and orchids he lavished on you," drawled Brooks. He was basking like a happy tomcat in the worshipful glances of Mrs. Sorpende, who had a penchant for swashbuckling heroes of high romance.

"I did tell horrible lies, didn't I? But it seemed the quickest way to make her face the truth, and he really is an awful old letch. Leila Lackridge always said so, though I couldn't believe it at the time. Poor Dolores, I suppose she was in love with him. The police won't do anything awful to her, will they?"

"What's to do? We can testify that she was duped, and she's turning state's evidence, of course. Anyway, she's sure as hell going to get all the publicity her heart could desire out of the trial," Max answered.

"I should think so! This must be one of the biggest art swindles ever hatched. I wonder if the other trustees are going to do anything about trying to get the originals back?"

"I'll tell you later. I've been asked to attend an emergency meeting at the Madam's this afternoon."

"Oh." Sarah sounded deflated.

Bittersohn glanced at her curiously. "What's the matter?"

"Nothing, really. It's just that they must be planning to offer you the job and — well, you know I have no car any more and I was planning to spend quite a lot of time this summer out at Ireson's Landing. Knowing you have family there, I was rather hoping to hitch a ride with you now and then, but if you're going to be traveling all summer — "

"Oh, I doubt if I'll be going anywhere yet awhile. A thing like this will take time to organize, you know. I'm sure we can work something out."

He smiled and Sarah turned a becoming shade of rose. They would no doubt be able to work something out.

"I wonder if they plan to close the museum?" said Mrs. Sorpende.

"They'd be smarter to keep it open and charge admission to finance the recovery," Brooks replied. "The fakes will no doubt be a bigger drawing card than the originals, at least until the publicity dies down. It's strange to think none of this would have happened if Palmerston hadn't got the wind up about Witherspoon's noticing his sweetheart had changed. Nobody else was taking poor old Joe seriously."

"Thus conscience doth make cowards of us all," said Mrs. Sorpende, who read Bartlett's Quotations a lot.

"That's it exactly," Bittersohn agreed. "Palmerston's curse was his imagination. Odd, isn't it? To look at him you'd think he hadn't a thought in his head beyond the Dow Jones averages, but dreaming up that fantasy about the vault and keeping Mrs. Tawne convinced of its reality all these years took downright genius, of a sort."

"Those champagne toast and the speeches," sighed Sarah. "I do feel for that woman. To me that was almost the worst thing he did, keeping poor old Dolores's nose to the grindstone so that he could play the shining philanthropist and at the same time throw away fortunes on a series of women who didn't give two pins for him. He's no better than a — " Sarah was still too proper a Bostonian to say precisely what Palmerston was no better than.

"Anyway, Brooks, now that you're out of a job you can move in here and help Mrs. Sorpende run the boarding house while I'm out at Ireson's farming. Mr. Lomax and I are going to plant a huge garden and grow enough provisions to last us all next winter. Mrs. Sorpende, you will quit that silly job in the tearoom and take over for me here, won't you?"

"I think the job is about to quit me in any case. The venture has not been a success. Yes, I should be delighted to assist you in any way I can. You know that, dear Mrs. Kelling."

"And what would I do?"

"You'd pay a thumping big rent, for one thing, which I'm sure you can well afford. And you'd do all the odd jobs Alexander used to do: putting new washers in the faucets, touching up the paint, doing something about that leak around the skylight, fixing window blinds so they'll roll. I hadn't realized how much tinkering it takes to hold an old house together. Everything's falling apart and I can't afford to keep calling in repairmen. We need you, Brooks."

"Yes, but how would Theonia feel about having me around? After all, I did help catch Palmerston and" – he shot a piercing glance from under his neat gray eyebrows – "he was mighty gallant to her."

Mrs. Sorpende caught a drip from the spigot of the coffee urn in a coin silver spoon. "I find myself quite without sympathy for Mr. Palmerston," she replied in her queenliest manner, "not only because of his dastardly wrongdoing but because of his offensive conduct toward me personally."

"Why? What did he do?"

"On the way back from the museum in his ill-gotten limousine, he made what I shall only describe as an improper suggestion."

"The infernal rotter," cried Brooks. "Why didn't you tell me, Theonia? I'd have dealt with him."

Mrs. Sorpende turned on her cavalier a gaze so tender that he almost swallowed his coffee cup. While he was choking and stammering, Mariposa came in with the morning paper.

"Hey, get a load of this," she shouted merrily.

They all crowded together to read. The lead story was on Palmerston's arrest, but there was another front page headline, MORE

DRAMA AT THE MADAM'S. A group photo showed two uniformed policemen, Lupe, Bengo, the watchman who'd been locked in the washroom, and Brooks smack in the middle looking like the cat that had virtuously refrained from swallowing the canary.

Sarah began to read aloud. "'Through the alertness and daring of museum guard Alexander B. Kelling' – why, Brooks, I'd forgotten your first name is Alexander."

"Of course it is. About every fourth male child born into the Kelling family since Hector was a pup has had Alexander stuck on to him somewhere. That's why I never use it. Why are you goggling at me like that?"

"I was just thinking that if I – make a change – and you get married, then there'll still be a Mrs. Alexander Kelling running this house."

"Well, yes, if I ever manage to land myself a wife."

"Cousin Theonia said she'd be glad to help out. Didn't you, Cousin Theonia?"

A smile of ineffable sweetness crept over the stately countenance. For a long moment Theonia Sorpende sat perfectly still, the silver teaspoon poised in midair. Then in her most dulcet tone, she spoke. "As you know, Cousin Sarah, my one great joy in life is to be of service to you and your loved ones."

"Damn it, Theonia," sputtered Brooks, "She's not asking you to darn a tablecloth. Don't I represent anything more to you than another odd job?"

Like a carrier pigeon flying home to its loft, a dimpled white hand fluttered into the eager grasp of Alexander Brooks Kelling. "Shall I tell you," cooed Theonia Sorpende, "what you mean to me?"

Sarah rose and beckoned Max and Mariposa out of the dining room. As they departed, a joyous drumming as of wings beating on a hollow log came to their ears. It was the mating ritual of the ruffed grouse. Cousin Brooks was proposing.